STARS

by

John Behardien

Duncurin
Publishing

Duncurin.com

i

DEDICATION

For Frankie, Emmie and Lottie, with whom I share those 'Fabienne' moments, and so much more. With all my love.

WITH THANKS

My sincere thanks to the following very talented people.

Hayley: Proof Reading and Editing hbr@proofedit.co.uk

Jamie Runyan: Another super cover design@reese-winslow.com

Yen Baet: For an amazing cover image Yen@yenbaet.com

CONTENTS

Chapter I

Once in a Lifetime

There it was, once again, the sultry glow emanating from those eyes of living crystal as she gazed at him. His heart resonated with that radiance; a fact he tried desperately to conceal. He set down the local paper that he'd been pretending to read: he knew, as soon as she sat next to him, the enquiry that would form on those pretty, sensual lips. He did his best to look surprised whilst she uttered the question he'd heard and answered a hundred times before, but couldn't quite prevent the smile from breaking through, just as she began to speak.

'Tell me again, Matt?' she said softly in almost a beseeching tone.

'Tell you what?' he offered redundantly.

'You know.'

'No, I don't. Mind-reading is not one of the skills I have acquired, as yet.'

'Think so,' she nodded convincingly, 'at least when it comes to reading *my* mind,' came the deep melodic voice that now extended to its lowest register as she assured him otherwise, and continued. 'So, go on then?'

'Go on what?' he teased just for a minute longer.

She perched next to his sun-lounger, like a child about to hear her favourite fairy tale one more time, with no less wonder now than the first time she'd heard it. 'Go on, Matt, and I promise not to ask you again… at least not for the rest of the day.'

He looked out at the calm, blue azure of the sea. He understood the appearance of the sea merging with the sky to be an illusion, but he could just make out from the fantastic panorama before him the curvature of the earth. Its enticing reflection unable to outshine the intense gaze that now held him dead centre, which was just as well: he realised that this was the precise centre of his own universe, of his life, of his very existence. His last but futile protest, as he sighed, doing his best but failing, as always, to signal that she had disturbed his quiet solitude whilst he read his paper.

'Okay then,' he capitulated. He looked steadily at her, as might a headmaster about to read the report of his brightest pupil whilst trying desperately to curb his own enthusiasm from growing, as it always did when he faced such a request, or even a glance, from those mesmerising blue eyes; the bright smile upon which his entire consciousness orbited. This tale had begun many years before; in point of fact, even before he had met the sensational pop star; she who had just been voted the sexiest woman on the planet for the third time; one whose beauty could not even be hinted at in the most fully-featured and vivid of dreams. The woman who one would have to see, in person, up close, as he could now, before ultimately realising that she was far more attractive, more beautiful and desirable than any static or dream-inspired image could ever convey.

'All right then. You want to know about my new surgery roof don't you?' As he offered the slight tease, a flicker of disappointment appeared on the pretty face staring at him. To

2

Fabienne's credit, unrepeatable thoughts with regard to what she'd do with his surgery roof, in that instant, appeared only fleetingly whilst her mind moved quickly on to frustration.

'No, *you know* what I want you to tell me about! Go on, Matt!'

The effulgent eyes now held him in their deepest and most entreating embrace from where he knew, even his tease could not rescue him. He returned his own cobalt-blue gaze, which met hers perfectly at that moment of release. Accepting that he'd reveal anything from his deepest, darkest secret upon which his life depended, or simply whatever it was that she felt she wanted to know—as now.

'You want to know about the CDs, don't you?' he confirmed.

He was rewarded at his point of confession with that wondrous smile, which, even now, caused his mouth to dry and his legs to tremble.

'The CDs, Matt,' she said as she nodded, contentedly, her girlish, fascinated gaze rising on her face, easily and typically.

'Well, I threw them all in the bin.'

'Go on,' she said, sensing he hadn't quite got over his need to tease her just a little. This was especially the case when he was faced with the more touchy-feely stuff she knew with which many men were uncomfortable; sensing a little more encouragement was needed. 'So, *why* did you throw them in the bin?' she prompted.

'I threw them in the bin…' he offered, as he tried to delay the words that would come next.

'Yes?' still nodding.

'I threw them in the bin because I was frightened.'

'Frightened? Go on.' She nodded, now with still more delight rising on her expression, sensing that he was moving towards the subject of which she would never tire.

'Frightened that I was losing my mind.'

'And were you? Losing your mind, I mean?'

'I thought so, for how could anyone think so much, care so much, dream so much and want so much someone they'd never met?'

A warm glow fired like the apex of the flame from a Bunsen burner, just as it reached its hottest temperature. She gazed at him, now speechless, whilst continuing to hang on the words she'd heard a hundred times already, with the exception of the tiny pieces of information he revealed each time he told the inexhaustible, compelling tale about the CDs.

The same day she'd come for him—now almost three weeks ago—when she'd whisked the GP away to her retreat in Barbados, having been unable to contain her enthusiasm for the answer to her questions about the CDs and, in point of fact, a million more things they'd discussed. Endless talks having taken place in between, relaxing and swimming, together with two of the things that she'd promised him on his list of sex, drugs and rock 'n' roll.

'So how could someone think so much, care so much and dream so much about someone they would never have met?' she asked as she rested the pert chin on a slender arm.

'That's the easy one. My feelings for her had crossed time,' he offered, unwittingly revealing that, he too, had thought of such things more than he would have wanted to admit.

'Crossed time?'

'Yes, ever since that day.'

'What day?'

4

He knew at that point just two things: firstly, that he'd said just a little too much; and secondly, that he couldn't help but keep talking because her fascination, curiosity and unabridged delight now depended on him speaking the words into which he'd incautiously strayed.

'That day I waited for her to emerge from the stars' entrance at the Palace Theatre in Manchester as I stood in that pouring rain.'

'Whoa, wait a minute! I remember that day! It was absolutely tippling but the concert had gone so well. You were there? You didn't tell me about that! I must have been a sweet and innocent teenager at that time?'

He ignored her questioning look, as always, fired by her fascination with just about everything that she saw and heard and touched and tasted. He continued with the futile hope that, if his next words were more enticing, she might just be deflected from further enquiry.

'I tell myself that my feelings for her were just so strong that I just had to cross time for her.'

'Why then,' she began, with just a hint of triumph on her face, 'did you throw the CDs away if you knew all that?'

He sat up as his deep-blue eyes stared at her unwaveringly so that she could look into his soul if need be, to judge the truth, or otherwise, behind his words. 'Well, I thought at that time I was either going mad or about to turn into some horrible stalker.'

She shivered a little, his words unintentionally reminding her of the stalker who, after gaining access to her bedroom, had strangled himself with a ligature tied around his neck.

Matt reached out quickly to hold her hand, recognising the painful thoughts being given life through memories that she fought desperately to subdue. He kissed her gently, trying to expunge those painful memories with a delicate touch. He knew, however, from the cries she gave in the depths of the night that the terrible sight that awaited her as she had returned home still haunted her.

He moved the conversation on quickly. 'Or, my feelings were so strong that they were simply pointing the way to my future.'

'Your future? You seem very confident of yourself, Doctor Sinclair.'

The look of false indignation appearing on her face, as he quietened quickly, was her revenge for him having teased her.

'What makes you think I'd want someone like you? Just because you're incredibly handsome, are easy to talk to, have a great body and are really good in bed? It's not as though you saved me and my career or anything like that, is it? It's not even that I fancy you. Not in the slightest little bit. I mean, I know that half the girls in Perrilymm are chasing you, together with similar numbers in all those surrounding villages.'

'Well, all I came for was a bit of sun and some rock 'n' roll.'

'That's not what you said last night.' She licked her lips, a sensual look overtaking her expression completely whilst gazing at him. Then she remembered another snippet of essential information. 'Still, I suppose for someone who hasn't had a girl for two years...' she concluded, whilst doing her best to remove any trace of delight from her voice.

'Who told you that?'

'Mary.'

'She doesn't know *everything* about me, you know.'

'Okay then, it was Stella.'

'Stella, in the hairdressers?'

'Yes. What she doesn't know isn't worth knowing, especially about that *scrummy* Doctor Sinclair.'

'Well, she didn't know about you—*Sylvia.*'

'That's only because I distracted her with wanting my hair cut short. I thought she'd faint when I asked her to cut it all off.'

'Yes, I always meant to tell you what a brave thing that was.'

'I was terrified, but I knew I had to move on, try something new—and quickly. Besides, it really helped me with my disguise.'

He caressed the silky threads of her glorious head of hair between strong but gentle fingers as he looked at her, now helplessly. Sensing that she'd teased him enough—at least for the time being—she returned his gaze. Typically, she picked up on something that she'd noted from their conversation and now wanted to revisit.

'So, you've crossed time for me?'

'Well, something along those lines,' he offered a little vaguely, as if not quite understanding the intensity of his own feelings. 'I prefer to think that, as soon as I'd heard about you, as soon as I'd seen a picture of you, I could no longer contain my own feelings. Emotions that were so strong that time itself couldn't contain them. Either that or I was going mad.'

'Yes, I suppose if I'd known how you felt when we met in Luciano's, I would have been a teeny bit scared.'

'Scared? I was terrified. Steve was convinced he was going to have to section me, or at least put me in special measures where my practice was supervised!'

She laughed. 'Yes I can see now. Is that what he was pressing you about when you were talking in the kitchen the day he invited us to dinner?'

'Yes, yes, I knew I couldn't reveal just how you'd ended up at my house. He would have me carted off before you could say, *"Sit down and have a glass of wine, Steve"*! I also reckoned that I could never reveal, either to him or to you, just what I thought about you, so I just had to play the star-struck fan.'

'Which you did very well,' she interjected.

'Or *you*'d have called the police and also had me carted away!'

'Yes, I can see now it was a bit of a high-risk strategy for you. So how was it going to end?'

'That's easy. I had promised myself—and Steve—that once we'd met, that would be it. I would keep my promise to him and to myself. And that would be the end of the matter.'

'And would it? So that was it? Were you just going to give up at that point?' she posed.

'Well, obviously not. You're here, aren't you!'

'Only because decent boyfriends can be hard to find,' she teased once more, and continued. 'So how does it end now?'

'Well, that I cannot possibly say. Would you like to talk about something else?'

She had learnt to recognise that look in his eyes, the one that signified something that involved very little talking.

'I don't know about not having a girl for two years, you're more like a man just out of prison!'

'You didn't complain last night or the night before?'

'Who's complaining?' she managed, just before falling into the strong arms that comprised his gentle but passionate embrace.

The following day she dragged him out of bed especially early, which took a couple of sharp tugs on the duvet, but eventually her girlish enthusiasm, as infectious as always, roused him. Fabienne had insisted on showing him round the island and sharing with

8

him some of her favourite places. Two days before, on another early start, they'd taken a submarine voyage under the clear waters off Barbados. Viewing the coral reef and other sights, illuminated by a strange green-glow from the filtered sunlight twenty metres below the surface, she'd pointed repeatedly at the strange sights whilst she stared, mesmerised, looking on through the portholes, her manner resembling that of an excited little girl whose delight on Christmas morning was now just as compelling as it had been on going to bed the night before.

She drove him to Bridgetown docks where a sleek, impressive catamaran awaited them. The craft was silhouetted against the bright day and gleaming seascape; the sun beginning its ascent of the vivid blue sky, like a cherry rising to the top of a curacao cocktail; losing its redness as it rose, in exchange for unremitting power. Running ecstatically along the gangplank, her animated gait seemed to resonate with the spring in the wooden boards, whilst she looked round repeatedly to see that he was still following.

The captain met them on-board and made sure their personal effects were stowed before leaving them to make themselves comfortable on the large boat, which they had to themselves. Within minutes he steered the beautiful craft carefully from the harbour entrance under stuttering engine power. Upon passing the harbour wall and entering the open sea, he then unfurled the motorised sails. The vessel slowed and quickly became silent as the engines were switched off. The captain timed his move to perfection. There was a slight pause. Then, in a sublime moment, the great expanse of white sail shimmered and flapped a little against their mountings as they luffed before the breeze and against the intense blue sky. Suddenly, the sails filled with a constant following wind, which seemed to grip the craft, transforming her: she almost flew with fleeting contact of the waves at speeds approaching 40 knots. The skipper pointed the vessel north, locating remote sand-lined bays where turtles swam unmolested.

Upon anchoring in a calm, deserted sandy cove, they were able to snorkel from the back of the catamaran, the blue waters a little fresh due to the sun's absence overnight, but not cold. Before entering the water, Fabienne advised him to leave the bright watch behind, just as she did hers, lest Barracudas attacked the silvery reflection, thinking it was a shoal of fish. The turtles seemed completely unperturbed whilst the couple kept their distance, observing their calm and determined progress without interruption. Despite the Perspex mask, he could make out the smile that continued to dance with delight on her expression.

They ate a packed lunch Fabienne had prepared with a little help from Matt. He'd done his best to intervene without upsetting her, knowing that the pop star could halt galaxies in their progress around the universe with her music, but who had much lesser abilities when it came to the preparation of just about any food. Mercifully, the provision of food involved more assemblage than cooking, and even she could not spoil pre-cooked and pre-packed food. They spent the rest of the morning sitting on the deck. The captain moved his boat further north along the calm waters found on the west coast of Barbados, which was not subject to the rolling Atlantic swell, so typical of the eastern seaboard.

In the afternoon, the sun seemed to dip ever faster towards the horizon whilst offering a magnificent blazing sunset to illuminate the lovers with its ruddy and warm hues. They stared, mesmerised by its beauty and the palette of colours it displayed as it slipped ever lower from the undisputed position it had occupied in the sky a few short hours before. The captain brought the boat about.

Once In a Lifetime

Once again, the sea breezes seemed to give flight to the acres of sail in the jib and main sail as the craft skipped over the waves, journeying south and back to its moorings in Bridgetown. The couple sat right to the front of the boat, seemingly suspended in mid-air, whilst the sea rushed beneath their feet; sliced between the twin hulls of the wonderful vessel. The billowing sails ensured that the craft soon picked up speed, promoting the illusion that they were flying over the waves rather than remaining in contact with them.

She rested her cheek on the smooth cable that ran across the beam on which they sat. The trampoline that ran between the hulls lay aft. Cresting waves surged excitedly below them with some phosphorescence, coming from the angle of the sun as the sleek hulls cut through. Upon turning her head away from the spray she looked directly at him. Surging thoughts crystallised into a more coherent pattern as she spoke. 'Are you happy, Matt?'

Her gaze now focused unswervingly on him. The look that could support continents, held the promise of a blue dawn filling the eastern sky, kept oceans on the move and retained planets in their orbit, now fired with the one burning question. She need neither ask nor say any more: she knew the answer that lay within those steady blue eyes. Much more than this, she recalled his expression she'd witnessed the day they first met as he gazed star-struck at her when she approached him as he sat nervously and tongue-tied in the restaurant in Salford Quays—although she'd never revealed, neither to him nor even to herself, what she now knew. This is why she'd elected to escape to his house in that beautiful village as she realised, at a subconscious level, what she now recognised with more force: she was really coming home that day.

The delay allowed a slight pause in her surging thoughts. Using this to kiss him again and look at him, she knew that the answer to her question was identical to the reply she'd give.

'Sylvie, I am on the far side of happiness, and I have a feeling that you know that. Are you happy? May I ask?' Only the slight hesitation betrayed the fact that he still hadn't got over the fact that he, Matt Sinclair, was on holiday with the world's most gorgeous woman.

'Can anyone die of happiness? Can you suffer an overdose?' she asked in all seriousness. The emotion growing so strongly within her had caused her to wonder just how it could be sustained.

He paused again, a little surprised by her answer. 'No, I don't believe you can, Sylvie.' His mouth dried, his heart fluttered, his palms moistened. Despite recognising these signs within, he still hadn't grasped the enormity of what they were discussing.

'Very well then, I am ecstatically happy, and I have been since the first day I met you,' she confessed at last. 'So, how does it end?' she repeated, picking up, as was her wont, from the conversation of the day before.

'How would you like it to end?'

She smiled again, his thoughts seeming to resonate with her own. It had come to no surprise to either of them that speech was only one of the means by which they could communicate. For some days, she had known precisely what she was going to say at this point. However, there was one final answer she sought. 'You know, Matt, don't you, that we don't need to go back… We could stay here?'

'Forever?' he had to ask.

'Forever,' she offered without a blink, a gasp or a miss from her steadily beating heart.

She understood, however, that remaining in Barbados would diminish him. Much of what made the man was his sense of duty, his need to serve, to work for his patients and to be an excellent doctor; the one who was all but worshipped by his patients. Although she had to ask her question once again, she already knew the answer. She also knew that, not unlike the first taste of the fruit of the forbidden tree, they could not remain indefinitely in the Eden that had only been allowed to exist both fleetingly and tantalisingly.

Matt somehow couldn't find words, and so she supplied her own answer.

Who could have blamed them if they had both grasped the tempting life she had dangled in front of them; simply to retire and never have to worry about work, stress and helping others. Ultimately, knowing that the forces that motivated him were not dissimilar to those that drove her, and that they would clarify their destiny.

'I know. Don't say it. You'd miss Missus Simpson and your new roof.'

He laughed. 'Not to mention my adoring patients.'

'And all your ex-girlfriends.'

'My friends, perhaps.'

'All those who lust after you.'

'People who depend on me.'

She accepted his conclusion: it was identical to the one she had arrived at herself, albeit with different examples. This settled, allowed her to voice a more momentous suggestion that, she realised, had been forming for more days than she'd have liked to admit.

'Well then, in that case, there is only one thing to be said.'

'Oh, yes?'

'We need to make a phone call.'

'A phone call to whom?'

'To Doctor Fergus Worthing.'

'The locum?'

'Yes, we need to know if he can cover you next week.'

'We do? Next week? Why? I thought we were headed back?'

'It's time, Matt,' she nodded with a certainty that could be detected, without using mind-reading skills, by anyone who had received the shortest of glimpses of the couple. The pretty face generated a look; a look that temporarily caused the sun's transit of the afternoon sky to be halted, for the heavens bore witness to the events that were about to be unleashed.

'Time for what?'

'Time for *us*. Time for *you* to make an honest woman of *me*. What do you say?'

'I thought you'd never ask,' he began, wanting to say other things before realising he couldn't contain what came next. 'I love you, Sylvie.'

'Half the girls in the village say you told them that,' she replied, the tease just too tempting to resist.

'Well, if I did, I was mistaken,' he suggested.

'And now?'

'Never been more certain of anything in all my life. Yes, please, Sylvie. I realise I'd never experienced love until I met you. My very being has crossed time for you, and I never want to be with anyone else.'

'Well, then, I suppose that will have to do if you can't think of anything *really* romantic to say. Come on, let's make some arrangements, if you feel *that* strongly about it.'

He looked at her, an expression of pure unabridged passion appearing on his face.

'Okay then, we'll phone them in an hour or so.' They sank back onto the trampoline, suspended between the hulls as the water ran by just a few feet beneath them.

She fell into his strong arms and knew that she could never be with anyone else. 'Whoa, steady on, boy! That poor captain will go blind if we don't tone it down.'

'Whoops, I thought he was too busy steering his boat. Mm, I guess just a glimpse of you in that bikini would be enough to distract any man from steering his boat.'

'Later then, Matt,' she suggested, passion replaced temporarily by a hug as the sun dimmed in the western sky.

The tempting offer faded quickly across the ether. Neither the descendant glow from the sun nor the scintillation from the waves on the sea could retain it. She knew he would never want to not be the doctor and the person he'd become over the past 28 years. Moreover, she knew she could never ask it of him any more than he could ask it of her.

He almost accepted her offer. In truth, he could never reveal to her that he almost said, 'Yes, let's stay.' In the days ahead, both would come to regret their decision. If only he had accepted her suggestion that they not return. She would, in that moment, have saved them both from the destruction that was about to come their way. Even the waves, swooshing and foaming, being dissected by the sharp twin hulls, seemed to be whispering, 'Stay, remain here forever, forever in paradise.'

The highest orbits were often highly unstable, causing even the most resilient of craft to either fly off into space, departing at rapidly increasing speed for infinite oblivion, or alternatively crashing down to earth, only to burn within the atmosphere, leaving no trace beyond destructive wreckage. Very similar to the wreckage that was now about to sweep through their lives from which even their love could not save them.

CHAPTER II

MILLION HEARTS BROKEN

The next time that Mrs Simpson set eyes on her boss was on the televised coverage for the news, filmed at Manchester airport, as Fabienne's personal Gulfstream jet, flew in. Only close observers would have noted the carefully disguised shock on the manager's face: she recovered quickly, doing her best to convince Janice that she'd seen through the whole charade from the beginning. The manager insisted she'd known from the outset just who was in their midst. Janice looked at her suspiciously. She was only then beginning to see with more clarity the ways of her boss, and began to challenge the convenience of her recollections. The young receptionist remembered all too clearly the look of shock and surprise on her face when she'd matched the famous face to the image that had been in Dr Sinclair's room for some weeks; the day that the woman in the red cap had appeared, the letter in her hand, and had refused to depart. The manager, completely unabashed, continued to press her authority behind her assurances that she had been 'in' on the whole thing, having only kept quiet on directions from their boss. Scepticism rose once again in the younger woman. Sensing that discretion was needed, she decided not to force the issue at that moment, preferring to take Dr Stevens' lukewarm black coffee into his consulting room as she seized her opportunity between patients.

A few days later, Janice and Mrs Simpson each received a substantial rich-textured envelope by special delivery. Upon opening the resistant flap, they both drew out heavily embossed and gilded cards: their invitation to what was to be known as the wedding of the decade, overshadowed by only the fading memories of the Royal Wedding. The setting for the ceremony was announced as Cornwall. Many guests had to look up the unusual destination with surprise, which served only to enhance the excitement of all those invited. A third envelope was delivered to Greg Stevens. Janice took it personally into his consulting room. Her delight knew no bounds when he suggested they could perhaps attend together.

Dr Worthing had been approached by Lucy, Fabienne's personal assistant, and retained for a further two weeks to cover Matt during his on-going absence from the practice.

Though the time frame was short, excitement was intense. The venue had been chosen owing to the relative ease of limiting access to the island; by so doing, the bride, groom and guests would be protected from prying eyes. Notwithstanding this, the media were determined to cover the event in as much detail as possible. Reporters, journalists and TV crews found themselves checking into every available type of accommodation, some days before. Others appeared at dawn in an attempt to catch a glimpse of the bride and some of the famous guests on the day of the wedding itself. Accommodation had been booked in Marazion for all the guests before the venue had been announced. On the eve of the proceedings, Fabienne had been secreted away on the island of St Michaels Mount itself. A marquee was erected at the embarkation point on the mainland side of the causeway. Champagne and canapés were available, and a string quartet played as people assembled. Guests were ferried over the

18

causeway at low tide by specially hired DUKWs sprayed in white. Ribbons running from the bow of each completed the nuptial theme. These craft, first used as landing craft in the Second World War, were readily converted for use as wedding-guest transport. Their amphibious and sure-footed characteristics were ideally suited to ferry over the 80 guests.

Special permission had been sought and granted by the St Aubyn family for the service to take place in the Priory church; the 15th Century rose window illuminating Matt and Steve, his best man, whilst they waited patiently but self-consciously for the bride. Both men stood nervously at the altar as sunshine flooded in through the stained-glass windows. A wooden gallery rail had been erected in front of the east-facing square window, allowing more guests to be accommodated inside the Priory than the capacity intended originally.

The atmosphere in the small church held a quiet hubbub of excitement. However, the relatively small crowd was more meditative than exuberant: they recognised the deliverance of the bride from traumas that many still preferred not to even consider. The groom, too, had been through many of these events with her. It seemed fitting that he was the one who now stood waiting for her. The other fact that had escaped none who were present that day was just how many were missing—more than enough to fill the priory four times over. These missing legions represented those who had either turned their backs on Fabienne in her moment of need or those who had been more than willing to accept that she had indeed killed her lover in some perverted sex-game. This, unfortunately, being a more convenient assumption for them to make, rather than her being an innocent victim: the person who'd returned home, alone, in the dark to find the grisly sight of a stalker who'd killed himself in the ecstasy and ultimate agony of asphyxiation for sexual gratification.

Matt and Steve had taken one of the first transports over to the island, crossing the causeway some time before the surging, grey-green tidal waters of the sea had inundated it. Matt was consumed by last-minute anxieties, which had rather less to do with any doubt on his part but more to do with whether she would realise, at the very last moment, that just about any man on the planet would gladly replace him.

As the two men stood waiting at the altar, Steve whispered to Matt. 'I can't believe it. Here you are waiting for the sexiest woman in the world to come and marry you.'

'*You* can't believe it, Steve? Just how do you think *I* feel? Can two people share the same paranoid delusion? I keep wondering if the drugs are suddenly about to kick in and bring us back to reality!'

'Listen, my boy, you'll never need a drug for the rest of your life, 'cause you simply couldn't better this.'

Matt could only nod as the words sank in.

'Unlike me, of course,' Steve continued. 'I've taken beta-blockers and a couple of Valium just to steady my nerves!'

'Okay, Steve, better make sure you sit down on the journey back in case you wander off the side. That water was a little choppy when I checked a few minutes ago.'

Suddenly, they were interrupted by the uplifting tones of the organ as the background music changed to Handel's water music. Fabienne walked in slowly, her arrival reminding Matt of the first day that he'd seen her so close in Salford Quays.

She walked forwards with her father and stood next to Matt. He tried not to turn and stare but, somehow, couldn't help himself. It was a good job that he wasn't required to speak in that moment:

his eyes insisted that every ounce of available energy was directed through them; he gazed, spellbound at the vision before him. Not even the ivory veil could filter her wondrous smile, and only a slight shimmer from the delicate lace hinted at her nervousness. Matt, at this juncture, was strangely calm. Knowing for some time that his whole life turned around this very point, as might a beacon shining constantly and clearly in a vast wilderness that he had traversed. He'd never been more certain of anything than waiting, here and now, for the person who had meant so much for his entire life. Suddenly he gasped, for there she was, standing next to him. The person he had waited for—seemingly forever.

The service seemed to pass in a blur. Matt did his best to take it all in, and of course to respond appropriately at the correct time. In truth, however, he simply couldn't take his eyes off the girl who now stood next to him; the girl who'd come back for him when she could have been just about anywhere, with just about anyone. She'd chosen him. He found that the more he thought about it, the more nervous it made him. He needn't have worried: she exhibited not only that simple joy of life but, above all, a calm permanence that, in some way, now flowed to him. Each followed dutifully the instructions from the priest and made the responses at the correct moment. However, for the two people at the centre of events, it was almost as if a diffracted pattern of light shone around them, obscuring their view of anyone else. It was only as the service came to an end and Matt was asked to kiss the bride that some focus in the daydream had been restored. As Matt approached, he whispered, 'I crossed time for you, Sylvie, and I'll love you forever.'

'Only forever? I suppose that'll have to do.' She smiled as she leant in and hugged and kissed him to the delighted cheers from their guests.

21

Following the ceremony, Matt met Fabienne's mother, Marisse, for the first time. All at once, he saw the beautiful looks that had been passed down in good measure to Fabienne. In that moment, too, he could also see just how gracefully and beautifully the young bride would age. Marisse had brought her young consort, who seemed a little dazed by the proceedings. Although her father attended, having agreed only at the last minute to give away his daughter, he, too, appeared unsettled, but was at least cordial and polite. The atmosphere between he and his ex-wife, however, was strained, and soon after the service he approached his daughter to kiss her, shake Matt's hand, and departed without further ado. He made something of a sad and embittered person as he walked away, taking one of the transport craft back to the mainland as the choppy tide surged round the tidal island.

Only the official photographer was allowed on to the island. The packs of press had observed a respectful distance, having been encamped on the car park back at Marazion as the married couple returned on the DUKW, now bedecked with glorious ivory ribbon and bright flowers. Fabienne, as befitted her thoughtful style, had requested hot drinks and sandwiches for all those who waited for them. Though she and Matt came from humble beginnings, both were now—whether they liked it or not—right at the heart of celebrity status.

A larger reception awaited them in one of Cornwall's famous restaurants, the renowned chef having agreed to cater specially for the 150 guests who'd been invited to attend. TV cameras beamed live footage across the UK and to the world. Fans of the pop star, and those who had never quite given up hope that they would one day meet the star of their dreams, just as Matt had done, watched as wishes evaporated and hearts broke.

As is the way with things, however, not everyone was a fan of the bride, and a few could not even find it within themselves to wish the couple well.

Rita had watched the proceedings from her hospital bed. The consultant gynaecologist had just been dismissed by her, having the misfortune to deliver news of the worst kind. Unfortunately, the bleeding had been too vigorous to save the pregnancy. Even worse, however, was the fact that a hysterectomy had been required to stop his patient from bleeding to death. This was the only way to save her life and had been carried out as an extreme measure of last resort. Rita, as always unable to tolerate fools, held most vitriol for those who brought her bad news or simply anything she didn't want to hear. She'd shouted and sworn at him, asking him how it was possible that he was so incompetent, despite the sweat on his brow, the tremor and the exhaustion on his face, deeply etched with worry, giving more than a mere clue to how the poor man had fought not only to save the baby but also her womb as well. In scenes reminiscent of the Salem witch trials, the female GP had bellowed excoriating curses at him as he retreated through the door. The nurse, who attended with him, dissolved in tears: the words cut and whipped like a lash on their backs.

Rita watched the wedding with mounting distaste. As she continued to look at the glittering images, vengeful thoughts formed in her dark and desperate mood. Mr Farrington-Delver, senior gynaecologist, retreated hastily from the side ward, now with panic and fear joining his sadness and exhaustion. She'd saved the most chilling of her words until the very last, screaming at him that his surgical skills, such as they were, would henceforth only be used to cut up hot dogs in a rented burger stall when her solicitors had finished with him.

An observer of the patient might conclude that jealousy, fed by the desperately sad news, had created the black storm that now enveloped her, with Matt positioned at its centre. In a moment of clarity as those concluding televised frames came from the reception in Cornwall, Rita finally registered that before her was a picture of happiness. It was her understanding that the young couple resonated with something that, in her ultimate analysis, had eluded her all her life. By comparison, the existence she had built—and her presumed success—was nothing more than a pale facsimile of what the couple now demonstrated with each smile, each glance, and just about every nuance of movement and facial expression. The realisation in many would have promoted reflection or even learning. In Dr Letworth's case, however, only hatred came forth as a plan hatched quickly in her agile and inventive mind: to destroy the couple and replace their happiness with the sheer misery that now occupied all her thoughts unequivocally. Her mood deteriorated steadily as she watched the news: now she knew who was to blame for her misfortune and for the devastating turn of events that had rendered her childless, which had been the one thing that she sought above all else. She recognised the person who had robbed her of a chance of a normal life: the evidence lay before her in the images of the love-struck couple, who had surely created their happiness by destroying her own.

Some would argue that the hormones had brought to life such demonic thoughts; others would offer the theory that responsibility lay with the painkillers, the exhaustion or the anaemia. Still, others would conclude that, like a wire that had been stretched beyond its capacity and was about to snap with devastating consequences for all, quite simply, Rita had shouldered too much. However, she herself knew instinctively that the best way of getting rid of a bad mood was to pass it to another. She now understood that the same rules applied in respect of cruel and malevolent ones too. They would pay for what they had done to her.

As she watched more bright scenes, her clever but unhinged mind passed into darkness like a planet on its furthest trajectory from the sun as it entered a harsh and unforgiving winter. She threw a vase at the flat panel TV on the wall, as tears of frustration and pent up revenge were given vent. It fizzed and spat violently as both vase and panel shattered with a tumultuous crash that brought a terrified nurse running into the room.

Chapter III

Depth of the Night

Janice was in a dream-like state: she could not quite believe her ears when absorbing the suggestions made by Dr Stevens. The receptionist was on the distant side of ecstasy at the prospect of accompanying the young GP. She was not to be disappointed: the music, the venue and the atmosphere in the small priory were more than conducive to what she could only hope were two people falling in love. Perhaps even more vitally, her boss and the greatest rock star of her generation were the living, breathing proof that such things were not only possible, but alive, vibrant and well. She had borrowed money from her dad for the beautiful dress, which enhanced her bodily curves and slim legs. Stella had cut her hair beautifully. With one flourish, the hairdresser had banished the pigtails that had belonged to a little girl: in one deft move, the plain receptionist of old had, at a stroke, been replaced by an emerging attractive female. Her pale eyes doted on the handsome GP with the smooth skin, muscular build and deep velvety voice that seemed to resonate with calmness and sheer sexual allure that many women besides Janice had found irresistible. Though spellbound by the warm and impactful ceremony, at least one eye was kept firmly on her partner: this meant that she could respond in an instant to each nuance of mood as it crossed his handsome face and be there to provide a constant stream of gentle nods, adoring looks and, in quieter moments, delicate whispers in his ear.

After the reception, her sense of rapture was enhanced further still when Greg suggested they take a short walk along the seafront at Marazion, the kite surfers having long since departed for the tide encroached completely along the wide sandy beach. She thought that she was about to faint as they walked together, side by side, turning to face the wind to disguise the involuntary gasp she had been unable to suppress when he had suddenly and reflexly grasped her hand. Her whole body was trembling, which she desperately struggled to control.

Although her brain was completely overawed by the circumstances in which she had found herself, she knew that conversation was now needed to disguise her brimming emotions. Simple words would suffice. 'So, Greg, what did you think of the wedding?'

'I can't believe it. I don't think anyone can. It's almost as if we are all in a collective delusion and the alarm bell is about to ring on a special hospital ward for the very confused.'

'No, Greg, it's very real. I can understand how the changes in Doctor S took place over those weeks, ever since me and Monica Simpson waited outside his door as he took calls from Lucy, Fabienne's PA. I knew then, and I can see now, looking back, that something very special was in progress. I should have known the day Doctor Sinclair asked me to collect some files from his house and hundreds of press were camped out in his front garden! He played a really crafty game. I'd never have believed him capable of such a thing, although I suppose we could all rise to such a thing in order to protect those we love.' She took a breath, mentally applauded herself at covering up her wild emotions so convincingly. 'And you, Greg, are you settled in Perrilymm?'

'My goodness, yes. I've never been happier,' he said, the velvety rich voice extending to its deepest register. He looked at Janice, the happiness reflecting from his face, being readily received by her, whose delight in seeing such a sight knew no bounds. Then Greg uttered words that, it seemed, she, too, had been waiting her whole life to hear. 'Say, Janice, do you fancy staying over? We could head back Sunday night?'

Janice paused deliberately, checking her first instinct, which was to leap into his arms and place hers firmly round his large muscular neck. She knew, however, that the slightest of pauses could account for a great deal, and that the slight delay—that she'd barely been able to effect—would mask the extent of the passion she held for him.

A short time later, Greg's Mazda MX5 swept north from the car park at Marazion, towards St Ives, but then ran east as night fell to envelop the excited young couple. They booked into a small but comfortable hotel overlooking a quiet, unspoilt bay on Cornwall's north coast. During the evening meal, Janice did her best to eat slowly. Despite doing her best to control her surging thoughts, she was unable to resist staring at the young doctor more frequently than discretion would counsel. All her efforts at self-control, to slow things down and not to appear too eager, came to nought when she almost shot to her feet as they finished eating. He asked her if she would like a drink in the bar. Ultimately, mounting confidence caused her to simply grasp his wide palm and keep walking up to their room; no further words voiced. Inevitably, their bodies were entwined into the depths of the night as passion built and desire flowed. She held him as she wept with that release, now almost terrified of letting him go, as his strong, perfect physique unleashed forces within her again and again that she'd never experienced before in her young life.

Some time later, as she held him still more tightly, she whispered, just before sleep claimed him, that she loved him more than words could convey.

Matt and Sylvie drove to Exeter airport where, once again, the Gulfstream was fuelled and ready, awaiting their arrival. Twin jet engines screamed initially as the craft clawed skyward and then hummed satisfyingly as the plane gained mastery of the midnight, southern sky. The flight-plan logged for Nairobi. She snuggled next to him in the leather recliner. Nervousness, anxieties and unabated hopes that the day would progress smoothly now seemed to melt away as the two found themselves alone at last.

'Whoosh, that was exciting,' he ventured, extending a muscular arm to support her.

'More excitement than I can bear for one day,' she concluded.

'Well, hopefully we won't have to do it more than the once.'

'You are very sure of yourself, Doctor Sinclair. You know we rock stars: five bottles of champagne before breakfast and five husbands before thirty.'

'Well, Mrs Sinclair, I've been reading a book about being the most perfect husband, and I'm hoping to put my new-found learning to good use.'

'We'll see. A book, really? Where did you get up to?'

'The first chapter; not appearing to be too keen at your first meeting.'

'Fat lot of good that did you! You were *too* keen! You couldn't help yourself.'

'Well, it might just have something to do with meeting the most amazing pop star and the girl who's just been voted the sexiest woman on the planet—for the third time, I might add!'

'Well then. Can't believe all you read, you know.'

'Trust me, Sylvie, I believe it!'

'You say all the nicest things. Now where were we up to on that last kiss?'

'Let me see now, somewhere about here.'

They snoozed and chatted, but mostly they just enjoyed, basking in the new feelings of being united as a couple before their friends and, of course, before the church. Each of them realised that their relationship and marriage had been something of a whirlwind. Papers had postulated critically on today's precipitous duration of courtship that used to take months or years and now took barely a week or two. However, it came down to very similar feelings in each of them since each took the view that they'd found the person they were awaiting all their life. A long courtship where events were delayed solely on the basis that it may make them appear more cautious wouldn't have itself conveyed more certainty or security if things went badly. Fabienne had assumed that she would never embark upon a marriage: she had seen how two people who had once been so much in love could grow to hate one another. It seemed, when it all came down to it, that her feelings for her husband had been so strong that she concluded it was useless to either deny them or resist them—and hopefully they would face the future together where love would grow.

Nine hours later, the Gulfstream entered Kenyan airspace and landed at Nairobi. Kenyan time was three hours ahead, which brought them in at mid-morning. Being near to the equator, warm sunshine greeted them and enwrapped both of them like a warm blanket as they vacated the private jet. A smaller propeller plane awaited them as they arrived on Kenyan soil, which departed immediately for the Mara Serena airstrip in the Masai Mara, southwest Kenya. A Land Rover then transferred them to the private lodge that Lucy had booked for the honeymoon couple under what she hoped would be the protection of a false name: Mr and Mrs Clare. Neither Matt nor Fabienne had set foot in Kenya before, although Fabienne had played concerts in Cape Town and Johannesburg. Nonetheless, the wonders of the golden days—the awe-inspiring endless plains of the country with its ruddy, dusty ground and the magnificent wildlife—were not lost on the couple.

On the first night, she called him out on to the balcony, switching off the light as he appeared. Using her memory of his last position as a guide, she moved closer to hold his hands as unremitting darkness now flooded in. Only the calls of the big cats hunting in the dark and the bellowing of the elephants interrupted their quiet discourse.

'Tell me, what do you see?' she asked. She knew he would remember that first night; the night he'd saved her as they stood on the little wooden bridge with the smooth handrails, just beyond his back garden; the water, like black ink, flowing with barely a trickle in the depth below them. Long elegant fingers were deployed to frame the handsome face as she came even closer, staring at him in the near-perfect blackness. He smiled, for how could he ever forget that night: the night where instinct had formed a plan to allow him to check the misery and turmoil in which she found herself, the blackness existing just before midnight, all at once erasing that suffering, whilst the stirrings of a recovery had begun.

'What do you feel?' she whispered, pulling him still more closely as she felt his facial muscles form the deep, reflex smile

31

that visited his face easily. 'Now look up,' she entreated as she continued to stare at him through the inky-black of the night.

The absolute black of the Kenyan sky had been peppered with a billion stars that were now their only witness as their eyes received light that had flared and been sent on its journey millions of years before. She held him with a little more force, re-engaging with his line of vision. Each of them stood spellbound by the undiluted glory of the universe as unquantifiable scintillations occurred at infinity but yet seemingly resonated deeply within both of them.

'Will you come here again with me in fifty, sixty or even seventy years from now?' she asked, with something of urgency in her voice as it went up a semitone.

'Yes, of course, and beyond.'

As he approached even closer, their faces now almost touching, he could see the brightest stars of the galaxy reflected in those beautiful eyes that had long since dilated to their widest extent with unabridged awe as she took in the night and the person who had crossed time for her.

'Thank you, Sylvie,' he began.

'For what?'

'For this—for bringing me here to see all this, the magical night, the wondrous stars. And, of course, thank you for you.'

'Well, the pleasure's all mine, Doctor Sinclair.' She kissed him and fell into his arms as the blackness of the night seemed to envelop them. Stars a half million miles in diameter, burning with immeasurable forces, light years away, could not bear comparison as he held her gently but with a force that not even gravity itself could match.

CHAPTER IV

SOCIAL OCCASION

All too quickly the honeymoon was over and the Gulfstream warped north like a sailing ship of old against an invisible rope, the heading set for its base in Manchester, Ringway. Matt returned to the surgery the following Monday and began by thanking all his staff for the hard work they had invested during his absence. Though Matt, as always, did his very best to keep his mind on work, the fact that Fabienne insisted on accompanying him to the surgery on his first day back made it something resembling a social occasion. Only a Royal visit could have done more to excite the staff and the patients who wandered in, hoping to catch a glimpse of the pop star, and to welcome back their local doctor.

Special thanks were afforded to Greg Stevens for holding the fort and also Dr Worthing, who departed with some regrets: he had enjoyed his time in the little village and at the surgery, which seemed to have developed more with each passing day. Before leaving, he came to say his goodbyes and to pass on his congratulations to Matt. He shook Matt's hand and wished him well. Matt handed over a bottle of the finest and most sought-after single malt whisky. The locum's eye lit up as it was passed to him, and he couldn't help but think what a lucky man he was: he must, with certainty, be the man who had it all. Not only living an idyllic life in a heavenly village with wonderful patients, but also a wife widely regarded as one of the sexiest women on the planet. Dr Worthing saw with his own eyes why this idea was not without good reason when he'd glimpsed the star at close quarters that afternoon. She stayed to meet up with all the staff before departing for a concert at the O_2 arena. How could anyone better this? This must surely be perfection; nobody else's life could surely come close.

The building works had all but finished, and the surgery was now much larger with additional facilities: the new roof shimmered, resplendent in the morning sunshine that had finally managed to drive off the light mist and the remnants of icy rain. The local people and patients were generally delighted with the new surgery. The architect had visited a few days before and suggested an opening ceremony with their guest of honour not only now a local but also a world-class celebrity. He had departed with a little spring in his step and promised to return as soon as the celebrity couple were back in town so that he could ask them in person. The temporary accommodation had been disconnected from services and removed to restore the car park and adjacent ground that was soon to be landscaped. Clearing the car park in this way had opened up the vista from the surgery, allowing more light to enter the premises, thereby showing off the new improvements to greatest advantage.

Mrs Simpson had wasted no time in restoring the place. Contract cleaners had been engaged to sweep through the building from end to and. The manager had singlehandedly—after securing the go-ahead from her boss—interviewed and appointed new staff who were due to start shortly. Although there was still much to be done, before an opening ceremony could be even contemplated, the establishment had a more settled, finished feel to it, which staff and patients alike found reassuring. Matt was amazed at the transformation, and could now see a medical centre with every facility and a steadily expanding list, which he now realised he could serve much better with a little help from Greg. The results were beyond his wildest dreams. He considered that, whatever changes lay in wait for the small but growing surgery, given the breathless pace of change in the modern NHS, he was now more than ready to rise to the challenge.

One person stood out much more than the rest, and in his relatively short absence he could see transformation from the gawkish young girl into the attractive young sassy woman that Janice had become, encompassing an allure all of her own. Upon seeing both she and Greg together one day, the reason for this rapid change became apparent. Janice had also taken on new skills. Having enrolled in a night school class for web design, she approached Dr Sinclair to see if he were interested in entertaining a surgery website to go with the modern transformation that was sweeping throughout. Janice was doubly embarrassed when the GP not only embraced the idea but also insisted on paying her for the time it would take, and also offered her a bonus upon its completion. The receptionist's pale features still readily showed embarrassment, despite her newfound confidence. Her legs trembled as she tried to explain that the project would be part of her course. Matt simply smiled at her with no further discussion required.

Afterwards, the young receptionist had then produced a small digital camera and asked for permission to capture various images from around the new surgery that could then be used to enhance the web pages. With no further comment, but with more than a hint of a proud smile on his face, Matt made a few clicks on his computer. Turning the display round so that she could see the new and more powerful camera he'd just ordered. 'There, Janice. It should be perfect, and it will be delivered to you tomorrow.'

She left the consulting room with a mixture of delight and nervousness coursing through her brain. She realised that she was neither surprised nor disappointed. Her boss habitually backed both herself and any of the other staff whenever they went to him with requests and reasonable suggestions.

Matt and Fabienne soon settled in to a quiet life in the beautiful house on the edge of the village, although neighbours were curious about their megastar neighbour. In time they could see just what Matt could see: that despite her amazing talent and film-star looks, she was, at heart, just an ordinary girl.

Matt poured a painstakingly made cup of coffee, just the way she liked it. He used one of her favourite little pods from the tall, twirly rack, knowing that this was her favourite—and as it was *special* from last Christmas, a flavour that was now unobtainable. He'd warmed and frothed the milk and pre-heated her special mug. He placed this in front of her, together with two pieces of lightly toasted brioche, made by her favourite French bakers that he'd obtained on a special trip to the new supermarket that had opened in Media City, Salford Quays.

She smiled. 'It's not my birthday until April, you know.'

'I'll just get some orange juice, my darling.' He pressed the little button on the hi-tech machine. Oranges were fed automatically, passed from the little basket on top, and flowed down the twin symmetrical channels where the oranges were crushed, the fresh juice extracted, and the pulp separated in one smooth progression.

'Did you sleep well, Matt?'

'I did, Sylvie. Nothing beats one's own bed. Does the mattress suit you? We could change it if it's not to your liking?'

She smiled again and picked up the frosted glass that he'd extracted from the freezer, now containing the fresh juice he'd poured from the machine's reservoir. 'No, Matt, my love, it's just perfect, and so is your beautiful house.'

'I am so pleased. Here is the paper, my darling. Besides it's *our* house, Mrs Sinclair.'

'The paper, Matt? But you love to read the morning paper.'

'Oh, no, my love, *you* have it.'

She deliberately raised the paper, pretending to be giving it serious consideration as it hid her face. In that moment, however, the pent up laugh came that she could suppress no longer. 'Okay, I'll do it!'

'What, my love?' he asked carefully.

'You know full well, Matt Sinclair. You've been asking me for weeks. I'll do it, just for you, I'll do it. And remember when you are eighty-three, I'll still expect a breakfast like this every morning!'

'I love you.'

'You'd better! All the favours I do for you and your friends who need a helping hand. I just hope it's in a good cause. Something like this could ruin my reputation, you know.'

'I doubt that very much, my darling. I don't think that's possible.'

'I said, I'll do it, you can stop flattering me now.'

'That'll never happen,' he opined as he kissed her again.

'Leave it to me, Matt. Tell your friend we'll do it. I'll just make one or two calls.'

Chapter V

Tribute Act

Ken Peters surveyed the sorry scene. He'd done his best to make the school hall as attractive as possible, yet everything was so expensive. His secretary, Marion, had done wonders, he had to admit. She had helped the cleaners get the place as spic-and-span as possible, had printed hundreds of posters and handed them out to all the shopkeepers and pedestrians around Knutsford. Many said they would come, but Headmaster Peters was not so sure. These were difficult times and money was tight. He knew his school was the poor relation to the large private school just down the road. In truth, there was no comparison: they had access to seemingly bottomless coffers, and had every facility at their disposal. To be fair, they'd offered Mr Peters the use of their facilities, including the massive artificial turf, playing fields similar to the one Mr Peters was hoping to raise funds for tonight. He regretted his promise now, made during his address at parents' evening twelve months ago, and also to the governors: that he would improve the sports facilities at the school. He knew that he was still well below his target. Third-generation artificial turf with the superior infill of sand and recycled rubber was much more expensive that the older first-generation offerings. He'd been reliably informed that if he was serious about such things then this was the only option. Sadly, it was also the most costly.

He couldn't thank Marion nearly enough: she'd worked tirelessly. She had hired extra seating and the hall was now bursting to capacity—albeit with empty seats. She also managed to get a few more spotlights from somewhere, and heaven only knew where those large speakers had come from. Her massive coup was—she'd informed him—that she'd booked Zara Connolly to come and perform. Thinking with her appearance, they'd be able to charge ten pounds a ticket on the door. Mr Peters had never heard of Zara Connolly, but Marion, who was five years younger, had explained that she was a very popular Fabienne tribute band. Moreover she had agreed to appear for half her usual fee of five-hundred pounds. Of course, everyone had heard of Fabienne—but would people really pay to see a tribute to the real thing?

Mr Peters still couldn't see it stacking up somehow. Five-hundred seats at ten pounds a seat sounded wonderful. The cold shiver down his spine—one of pure embarrassment—told him that they'd be lucky to fill a hundred of those seats down there. Nevertheless, he was truly grateful to be head of West Knutsford High, and the pupils were generally studious and well behaved, he knew that they were 'also rans' in the modern world; a world where private schools as well as self-governing trust schools could outpace him at every turn.

His staff were hard-working, but results and their standing in the league tables were firmly set on 'average', and he recognised that this was unlikely to change. He'd hoped that, by improving the sports facilities, this would have a knock-on effect, and somehow represent a turning point. He wondered, now with more anxiety arising in the pit of his stomach, how an event that promptly flopped would affect morale. Marion's energy and enthusiasm seemed to be completely undaunted by the lacklustre return of interest slips from parents and local residents. She told him that he shouldn't worry, that it was a start, and nobody knew where it might lead. Even a thousand pounds would take them a little nearer to their goal. The headmaster didn't dare subtract the costs that they were about to incur from this humble figure.

He looked at his watch: half an hour to go. He estimated that there were about twenty people in the hall. Marion had placed a blackboard outside some days before, advertising in large block white letters, 'Fabienne Tribute, this Friday'. Well, here it was, Friday, and it was time for success or the ignominy of failure. His racing heart predicted, quite accurately, what he knew was about to unfold. Heaven only knew that she'd done her best—even having been in contact with the local radio and local newspaper, but they'd all shown little enthusiasm. Several had even asked her who Sarah Connolly was. None were prepared to either offer column space or send a photographer.

To make matters worse, he could hear a large truck in their car park. One of the local hauliers had asked some months ago if they could park one or two of their HGVs in the school car park over the weekend when the school was closed. Mr Peters had forgotten to ask them not to park this weekend, and now, even if some people did turn up, they'd have nowhere to park. He knew that the overwhelming instinct was to sneak home and pretend this simply was not happening. He knew that, despite his panic, however, he could not let Marion down. Whatever happened tonight, she had done her utmost, and it would in no way reflect on her.

Perhaps if he had been brighter, more energetic with enthusiasm or verve (whatever that was), the school wouldn't be in the mess it was now in. He hated failure, but he realised in that moment he only really had to look no further than the nearest mirror to identify the culprit behind this fiasco. He knew then, in that moment, that he would have no option other than to offer his resignation next week. As if his professional failure wasn't bad enough, he hadn't even summoned up enough courage to tell Marion just how he felt about her, despite the fact that she'd worked for him for over two years.

Another loud noise came from the car park. Now, absolute catastrophe, a large coach was pulling in. The hauliers had said they would need occasional space for parking one or two of their coaches. It was a complete disaster. Surely things could get no worse.

One or two more people had started to wander in, filling at least two rows, which that made about forty people. If they could get twice this number, they'd at least cover their costs.

Suddenly, music made famous by Fabienne started to issue from the speakers. Perhaps Zara could pull it off. All they needed now were some more spectators. Mr Peters knew deep down that they'd all have better things to do—and begrudgingly, he had to admit to himself, they would if they had any sense.

Without warning, the hall lights dimmed and intense spotlights flared. He was sure he could see a laser projector fire over the stage area, joined by bright stroboscopic lighting. This looked amazing and so professional. Marion had said that her neighbour's son would be able to work the lights and that they would cost no more than a hundred pounds to hire. He looked up at the wires, the supports and the electronics: it seemed like a massive amount of kit for the money.

He saw two young men appear on stage, both carrying guitars. Another girl appeared in a short black shift dress. Two men helped her with a keyboard. This was extraordinary because he was informed that Zara was a karaoke act and sang to a pre-

prepared tape. Perhaps she had upped her game. In any event, as Marion had promised, she was good value—especially at half her normal fee. What a bargain!

Even as the head continue to stare, more people filed in. Three young women in matching black shift dresses stood at the back of the stage. A spotlight found them.

Microphones were brought in and others wearing black T-shirts and black jeans appeared, plugging these into large black boxes that had appeared at the side of the stage. For a moment he thought they might be backing singers, but what would a karaoke singer need backing rhythm for? Further microphones were placed in front of the girl with the keyboard. Men, all dressed in black, continued to bring in equipment, and next a full set of drums appeared. The more he watched, the more the scene changed. More musicians appeared, alto sax, double base, trumpets, French horn and four violinists. The stage was now crowded with musicians. He was about to eat his words: Zara was no doubt much bigger and better than he'd thought possible. Strange he'd never heard of her. He supposed that on the pop scene these days most were half his age. People in the audience now had their phones out and were madly texting. Mr Peters knew they could sense a bargain just as he could.

He decided now would be a perfect time to go and find Marion. 'Marion, goodness me! This seems a big act. I've never heard of Zara Collins but she must be a pretty big star to command such resources. How does she do it for the money?'

'Just as I said, headmaster, I explained our dilemma that we were hoping to improve our sports facilities and were looking to raise at least ten-thousand pounds. Her agent said she would appear for half-price.'

'But Marion, all these people… They can't be cheap.'

'Oh, you know, just a few out-of-work session musicians. No doubt they have turned up for a few pounds.'

'But they seem so professional and the kit they are bringing in seems first-rate.'

'I suppose Zara knows what she is doing.'

'And the lighting is a neighbour's son, you said?'

Marion paused for some time. She was bursting to tell him a little secret that she'd been keeping for a week or two.

More and more spectators started filing in. Some had obviously rushed here. They, too, could sense a bargain.

In that moment, a microphone was placed centre-stage and plugged in with all the other now highly complex electronics. The music grew louder. Flares and smoke were fired from canons that had been mounted on stage. Mr Peters had never seen anything like it. It was almost as if they were at a professional concert.

More lasers fired, smoke flares went up, and a steady beat began to emanate from the young man now sitting behind the stack of drums. Two other men filed in at this point, positioning themselves just in front of the stage. They had on reflective jackets and small curly wires inserted into their ears. Mr Peters thought with a laugh that they looked like security, but since when did Zara need security? And why oh why had no one ever heard of her?

In the blink of an eye, a young woman appeared on stage. The lights fired in a focused pattern, all on her. She wore a black hooded cloak, but more than a glimpse of a really short silver dress in a shimmering fabric was revealed. The impossibly long legs sported vertiginous spiky heels. Mr Peters wondered how she could walk in such footwear. The audience seemed numb. More and more started texting quickly but silently, as if they were collectively holding their breath. All now stood open-mouthed,

Tribute Act

watching this amazing young woman whose face remained in the shade, courtesy of the large hood. He wasn't surprised that they were texting: even when shrouded in the black cloak she looked absolutely stunning.

Numbers were swelling in the hall; there must be nearly sixty people down there. Many of the men in particular were on their feet, but the two who'd been standing at the front seemed to step forward and encouraged them to sit down. More and more filed in. They also asked them politely to move up so that no spaces were left in the seating. Mr Peters laughed but could not fault their optimism. The background music from the speakers quietened, and the woman on the keyboard began playing what could only be the young artist's signature tune as she stepped forward to the microphone. At this, more and more of the instruments joined in, creating a rising crescendo. She strode to the microphone, and silence suddenly descended across the entire hall as the sense of anticipation reached a climax.

Marion had joined him again but quickly made her excuses. The headmaster saw that the hall now contained at least a hundred people. They were saved! What he couldn't see were the people queuing at the main entrance and down the path that led to the school.

Marion joined Elspeth, her assistant, at the front desk.

'Marion, help, please! Where have all these people come from? They say the word has gone out there is a megastar in there. I thought it was Tara Cullen or whoever, someone I've never heard of! There are trucks and trailers out there. It's like the *O2 Arena*—not a local high-school!'

'Elspeth, please forgive me, I'll explain later. Now, how are we doing for tickets?'

44

'They're selling so quickly! I think we'll sell them all, with more still arriving. Even the pupils have returned. Have you ever known that?'

Marion thought quickly. She knew that in thirty seconds the hall would be full to capacity. She then thought of the large gallery rail that was usually occupied by the seniors during assembly. It completely encircled the hall, and a tiny section could be closed off above the stage for when school plays were in progress. She knew she had to move quickly.

'When you sell the last ticket, start allowing people upstairs on to the gallery rail. Tickets up there will be £20 each and pupils go free. If you see any of the more mature pupils then enlist them to help you to get customers, who won't find seats in the hall, upstairs. Cordon off the end section. I'll be there with the head, and the ones who help you can come and stand with us.

'You mean you're expecting even more?' Elspeth knew that the gallery rail was very large and would accommodate hundreds. She could see more arriving, but nobody had ever heard of the act they had booked.

Excitement gathered.

Suddenly, a large muscular man appeared behind her. She jumped as he stood next to her.

'Forgive me. We're here to help you, Miss,' he said pleasantly.

'Help me with what?'

'Crowd control.'

Elspeth felt faint. She wasn't quite sure what was going on. People queued steadily, more arrived; her moneybox was filled to overflowing. People almost threw twenty-pound notes at her, not waiting for change. She nodded with a faint smile, her mouth falling open, but somehow no words would come.

Another large muscular man in similar attire joined the first man. Both stood there as if they were expecting still more people to arrive. Both smiled at her good-naturedly as if they knew something she did not.

Marion re-joined Mr Peters at the end on the gallery rail as they looked down.

'My goodness, Marion, there are still lots of people turning up. I don't know how you've done it but it looks as if this Zara girl is more popular than I thought. I must apologise for doubting you.'

'No, that's not necessary,' Marion smiled, still looking a little guilty.

'But look!' The hall had filled rapidly. 'It looks bursting down there. I've never seen anything like it—not since I saw Santana at the Apollo in ninety-three!'

She smiled. 'Forgive me, head. I'll explain later.'

'There is absolutely nothing to forgive or explain. I just don't know how you've done it, and that girl, just look at her—she's amazing! It looks like she's just dropped in from Hollywood or Cannes or somewhere like that!'

Marion nodded to four prefects who were now patrolling the wings of the gallery rail at either side.

'I hope you don't mind, headmaster, but I've asked them to place more people up here. I have asked for twenty pounds a head, pupils go free.'

'You mean some of the pupils have come back? Well, that's a first!'

'Yes, indeed. I've a feeling it's going to be a night for firsts.'

The headmaster stared at the young artiste on stage, spellbound. Suddenly, the silence came to an end, the orchestra struck up again, and she allowed the black cloak to fall. The

46

young woman stood there, the crowd seemingly mesmerised. Mr Peters, too, could only stand and stare. In that moment, she turned and seemed to look upwards as if she were looking for someone. She waved to Marion, her long arms stretched well above her head, a stunning smile on her face that could stop traffic with its intensity.

'Look, Marion, she's waving! My goodness, she's waving to you. Wave back, Marion. Do you know her? My goodness she *is* amazing. How did you get hold of her? She looks like a million dollars.'

'Oh probably much more, headmaster,' Marion agreed quietly.

Suddenly the hall fell quiet again. The star clicked the microphone and she addressed the crowd.

'Good evening, West Knutsford High! Thank you so much for coming!'

The crowd went wild.

She waited; timing was everything, and the young performer had learned this skill.

Mr Peters stood amazed by her professionalism and the quality of the people around her. She was obviously destined to go far.

'For one night, only, we are *here*! And tonight we are here for *you*, for your school and to help with your fundraising.'

A wall of noise came from the crowd.

'Please be seated so those at the back can see, and let's begin, shall we?' She waited once again for the crowd to settle, but the music had already begun. The backers started up and the concert was underway.

Her melodic voice was projected to every part of the school, and the crowd swooned with delight. Mr Peters recognised the songs as being recorded by Fabienne, though he had to admit he'd never seen the megastar. However, judging by the performance of Zara on the humble stage below, she must be a frightened young woman if the tribute act was this good!

They were then joined by a tall figure who appeared on the balcony and stood next to Marion. He kissed her on the cheek. Mr Peters wondered who this man was who could kiss his secretary like this—the person he'd been in love with for two years.

'This is an old school friend of mine, Matt,' offered Marion. 'Matt Sinclair'.

Mr Peters was unable to respond for many seconds as he'd heard the name. 'Nice to meet you. Tell me, are you Doctor Matt Sinclair?'

'I am, but please call me Matt.'

'But, but, you're married to Fabienne…?'

'I have the honour,' Matt smiled.

The headmaster looked down once again at the mesmerising young woman on stage. He looked at the musicians she had brought with her, the backing singers and the leading-edge sound system. He shielded his eyes from professional lighting systems that were obviously being handled by an expert. He looked at the hundreds upon hundreds who were filing in, guided by school seniors and prefects; the sense of excitement, urgency and expectation written to each of their faces. Had he looked outside the school, he would have seen more men in hi-visibility jackets, marshalling traffic, with cones and temporary parking being set up under the watchful gaze of a few police. It had all been organised with almost military precision. He heard that amazing voice, and the crowd who were spellbound by its purity and power as they were transfixed by sheer delight. Who could have believed such a thing could happen in a local school—and one which, before tonight, had seemed on its last legs.

Mr Peters looked at Marion, who gazed back a little nervously, and then he laughed. He couldn't help himself from rushing to her and hugging her as he did the unthinkable and kissed her. Words flowed in an instant. The subdued lighting was barely able to hide her blushes. 'I love you, Marion. Who'd have thought you could pull all this off!'

'Forgive me, Ken,' Marion responded, 'but if we had advertised Fabienne herself as appearing, there would have been a riot. We couldn't have coped with the numbers. So the only thing was a low-profile start and allowing word of mouth to increase our sales.'

Ninety minutes later, Headmaster Peters took to the stage as the lights went up. His secretary had hurriedly handed him a wonderful bunch of flowers to give to their esteemed guest.

The hundreds and hundreds of people who had somehow managed to pack every square inch of floor space, both in the hall and on the gallery rail, were on their feet in ecstatic applause. News crews and professional photographers had arrived from the national newspapers, giving them the scoop over more local newspapers that had failed to generate any enthusiasm for an act they had never heard of.

'Miss Fabienne, I am speechless and overcome with delight. I cannot thank you enough for the amazing performance with which you and your team have honoured our humble school. I know that you play to packed venues, stadia and concert halls the world over, and I am unable to find words to express my gratitude on behalf of myself our staff, pupils and, of course, the school as a whole.'

Tribute Act

Tumultuous applause broke out amongst the crowds, and all on stage took a bow.

'Thank you one-and-all for sharing this amazing concert with us,' Mr Peters continued. 'I know that the evening has been a wonderful success on all fronts, and I am certain that we will now be able to carry out our promise to develop one of our playing fields: creating an all-weather pitch. Somehow, I suspect the school will not look back from this point on. So please, everyone, go from here with our best wishes, and tell everyone that West Knutsford High is back on the map with thanks to some very, very special people, who have helped us in ways beyond imagination, beyond ingenuity and beyond generosity.'

A further applause echoed around the hall, with cheers and whistles and shouts of appreciation.

'Lastly, I'd also like to extend my thanks to Marion, my wonderful secretary, and to Doctor Sinclair, who I expect have brokered a deal between, deservedly, the most famous pop star of our times and our humble facilities. I thank you all from the bottom of my heart.' He handed over the flowers and could not resist kissing the most fabulous woman, bar one, that he had ever set eyes upon.

Some time later, the headmaster and Marion waved goodbye to the famous couple who singlehandedly had gifted the school its biggest fillip that imagination could compass in one inspired move.

Marion turned to him and said, 'Did you mean what you said?'

'Yes, Marion, every single word.'

'*Every* word?'

'Yes, each and every one, including the ones most important of all. I love you, Marion. Forgive me: I should have plucked up courage to say that a long time ago.'

'Well, since you put it like that, it's better late than never.' She kissed him lightly.

'Things will be changing, Marion. We are going to give these larger schools a run for their money, and I thank *you*, most of all, for giving me the encouragement to think it can be done.'

'It was my honest pleasure, headmaster.'

The following day, Lucy Kwa, Fabienne's personal assistant, phoned to speak to the headmaster. She confirmed that Miss Fabienne's performance would be free from all charges, and that a cheque for ten-thousand pounds would be made available to the school, provided no mention was made of from where the funds had come.

Mr Peters could not help but hug and kiss his secretary, the girl whose foresight had made it all possible.

CHAPTER VI

SYMPHONY OF SPITE

Two weeks later, Rita returned to work with very different overtones. Plucking up courage, staff and colleagues approached her, wanting to express their sympathy. She quickly discouraged such talk by making sure that the perpetrator was made to feel so uncomfortable that they soon quietened and withdrew quickly, moving to other duties well away from the embittered female GP.

Sadly, hostility and the need for revenge had entirely displaced warmer emotions that might have, even then, banished very different vengeful ones that now consumed her like a gaping sore. The fact that the receptionists were abuzz with the events in Perrilymm and the proximity of a famous neighbour only served to focus the direction of such vengeance ever more keenly. Her intelligent and resourceful mind now formulated strategies that would give vent to the hatred and unabated spite that ran within her like a spring tide. Rita, however, was soon back in to the rhythm of her work, and few knew her well enough to detect the plans of destruction she was quietly honing to perfection.

She was showing her last patient of the morning to the door with her usual officious brusque style, having refused to provide him with time off work following bereavement. His father had passed away suddenly, and she had lectured him long and loud, the diatribe echoing far down the corridor, extending from her room and to the waiting room, her words berating those who wanted time off work for trivial reasons. The thoroughly chastened man shrank quickly through the busy waiting room, wandering past receptionists who had overheard every word of the conversation. He continued out into the more anonymous relief of the car park as he slunk away, his emotions in turmoil, his head in bits.

Had he looked up, even for a moment, he would have caught sight of a scruffy and dishevelled man pulling the belt a little tighter on his oversized and dirty brown trench coat. The garment was speckled with tiny ash burns cascading downwards from the thousands of cigarettes, and looked as though they had been tugged on with urgency—almost as if his life depended on them.

The rusty door was slammed casually yet aggressively, a loud shriek given off as the failing hinges and bare metal scraped together uneasily. The short middle-aged man went inside quickly and bypassed reception. He knocked just a little too loudly as he waited outside the door for the terse reply.

'Who is it and what do you want?'

The occupant stormed to her oak door, her temper causing her to open it forcibly and with more aggression than curiosity. Only then did an arch smile visit the face with the clear skin and bright green eyes that offered almost luminosity. She held the door open to allow him to enter whilst moving slightly obliquely around him, studying him like a cat about to pounce on unsuspecting prey. She wondered if this rancid little man could possibly be capable of undertaking the task she was about to demand of him.

Jim Duggan stood there, his weight a little diminished, his demeanour more nervous than his peers would have remembered; these characteristics brought on by his dismissal from the *Daily Scorcher* and the *Sunday Scoop*, following a purge by the owner,

Mervyn Boomer, who had dismissed many of the staff following Fabienne's successful action against the newspaper. Jim had been one of the first to be sacked, the bad news arriving by second-class post, notifying him that his mistakes had singlehandedly been responsible for the humiliating fines imposed by the Press Complaints Committee. Though the newspapers had reached an out-of-court settlement with Fabienne's lawyers, fines were reported to be the highest ever witnessed. Rumours were in wide circulation that the entire consideration had been passed immediately to charities. In a move so typical of the rock star, no credit was ever taken.

He sat somewhat defensively in the chair that she had offered reluctantly as she looked his scruffy form up and down with some distaste. Under normal conditions she would not have wasted even a glance in the direction of the disgraced reporter; however, these were far from normal conditions. Sharp green eyes bore into him as she scrutinised him. After some considerable delay, she decided she would take a risk and trust him, finally concluding that he was probably ideally suited to the plans she had hatched.

Such was the importance of the job for which she had selected him, she managed to suspend her normally terse and abrupt manner. Taking her time, she explained her plans in calm detail and with patience on her features—almost. Some moments later, she stood in front of him by way of summary.

He looked at the slim figure, the impeccable grey pencil skirt and the slim belt matching the black, glossy patent stilettos at the end of her shapely legs. Her revealing silk blouse shimmered, and she emanated passion as she clarified the strategy she had in mind.

'Now, do you know what you are to do?'

Jim nodded nervously, aware of the weight of her gaze upon him. He quickly slipped a cigarette in his mouth.

'Not in here, you fool! You'll have half the fire brigade out!' she instructed brusquely, removing her steely gaze from him as she glanced at the smoke detectors blinking steadily over their heads.

He tucked the crumpled cigarette behind his left ear. She looked even more distastefully at the dry, sallow and wrinkled skin that had suffered much more than age would have dictated, courtesy of the acrid smoke to which it was exposed on a more or less continual basis.

'Think I do, darlin',' he offered, trying to recapture his relaxed carefree style that had been lost some weeks before.

'You are to call me Doctor Letworth. Are we clear?'

'Yes, dar— Doctor,' he fumbled in response.

She caught his tawdry, almost covetous glance as he tried to direct his eyes to pierce the diaphanous silk blouse. Her well-honed and precise instincts regarding the minds of men was barely needed as she clarified the nature of the relationship that was to exist between them.

'This is purely a temporary arrangement until you have perhaps managed to plead for your job back and I have my revenge on the golden couple,' she advised, her tone now restored to its much more terse and clipped habitual timbre.

Jim licked his dry cracked lips with the first positive words he had heard in months.

'Did you manage to get what we need?'

'Yes, no probs, sweet… I mean, *Doctor*. Here it is, know all them sortsa people donn I.'

She looked at the clock on the wall. 'It's lunchtime. That's a good time now. You should be able to walk in. Make sure nobody sees you. Text me when you have delivered your little package.'

He held the tiny polythene bag up for her inspection. She nodded distastefully but knew that both he and it would serve their purpose—this being the only reason she was giving the malodorous little man the time of day.

'You'll also need this. Do you know what to do?' She held out the large blue zipped folder. 'Remember, you must find and remove one that looks identical to this. And, oh, wait a minute, these need to come off.' She pulled the orange security tags from the locks that secured the zips and handed it to him as a member of the aristocracy might hand over a lace handkerchief to some snivelling servant. 'You should locate two, remove just one, replace it with this one. Make sure you choose the lighter of the two and bring it back here. Can you do this?' She looked at him impatiently—the way she looked at most people—but also questioningly as she wondered if he was capable of having her trust—albeit temporarily—placed in him.

Jim nodded forcefully, checking himself from offering the typical strings of expletives that he would usually proffer at this point in discussions with most people.

She paused for a moment as impatience rose to an even greater intensity, Jim having failed to detect that their meeting was over. His mouth fell open as if he were waiting for more instructions. She turned away from him, signifying his final dismissal.

'When you are finished, come back here for another little job I have planned for you.'

Jim swallowed hard, opened his mouth again, but chose to say nothing. He placed the little bag in his pocket and clung on to the large blue zipped plastic folder. She didn't look back until some seconds after his departure, and then opened her window and the door to allow some fresh air to enter.

As she lowered herself into her chair, a cruel and intense smile made its way across her face as she considered the far sweeter smell of delicious revenge.

Jim departed the surgery in Perrilymm. His car growled into life as the exhaust issued black, acrid smoke and lurched over the speed bump as he drove away from the surgery. He wound down his window and spat out copious amounts of viscous spittle as a prelude to clearing his throat in order to accept another cigarette. He lit this distractedly as the car swayed towards the pavement. A furious young man, who realised just before Jim snatched at the wheel that he was about to be hit, shouted curses at the newsman as he swept past, Jim offering vulgar gestures in return.

Some time later, Jim approached the surgery and parked just down the street. As Rita had suspected, the place was very quiet. The GPs' cars were absent, and one or two receptionists were busy in the office. He crept in stealthily, pausing as he noticed a young receptionist with vivid red hair, her back to him. He proceeded carefully, like a husband arriving in late from the pub. She was taking photographs of the reception and the enlarged waiting area, her camera clicking enthusiastically as she fired off shot after shot of the improvements, recessed lighting and bright expanses of glazing that made up the new receptionists' windows. The flash fired several times as he continued to creep forward like a mouse under the nose of a sleeping cat. He knew that the 'stupid bitch'—as he referred to most women with whom he had contact—hadn't seen him.

Jim opened Matt's surgery door, which was typically unlocked. He stole in carefully, closing the door quietly behind him. He moved first to the beech desk with twin pedestals containing three drawers either side of a slim, central, wide one. He removed an old hanky, which was almost as dirty as his coat, from his pocket, and carefully wiped away any traces of fingerprints before placing the package in the lowest drawer on the right of the desk, opting for this one as it looked as though its contents had not been disturbed for some time. He closed the drawer carefully, doing his best to make little sound. He wasn't going to be stupid enough to leave any fingerprints.

For some time, he paced agitatedly around the consulting room, before eventually finding the two blue zipped folders he had been told to identify. He shook them both deliberatively; one was much lighter and still had the orange security tags present. Tucking this one quickly under his arm, he replaced it with the one Dr Letworth had given him. Within ninety seconds, he was back at the door, which he opened carefully, ensuring his exit was clear before quickly closing the door behind him.

Within the space of a few minutes, he had done enough to complete his mission and destroy the man whose happiness and career he'd been tasked to terminate in precisely this way. He thought, with a self-satisfied smile, that some jobs were easier and more rewarding than others—and things didn't get much better than this.

Walking briskly through the waiting room, he did his best to vacate the premises quickly. The stupid kid with the vile red hair was still concentrating on her photos and had not seen him—the stupid bitch. She'd soon be out of a job as well as that puff of a doctor. Jim now permitted himself the first grisly smile that had visited his craggy, smoke-suffused complexion for some weeks. He couldn't wait until he reached his car to light up with a sense of excitement and relief, spitting copious quantities of grey spittle

58

on to the newly laid block paving of the car park by way of some sort of calling card.

Jim drove back to Parkvale Health centre where the female GP awaited him. She sat behind her large desk as he carefully knocked on the door. 'Ts'all done, Doctor,' he offered with a mix of a sneer, triumph and curiosity. He grinned like a man who'd found a strange pill on a park bench and had swallowed it whole.

'Well done,' she offered brusquely, the slightest hint of warmth breaking her icy smile. She took the blue folder he offered and checked the security tabs. 'Excellent work,' she concluded, surprise now appearing like weak sun in the midst of icy wastes. Her instinct about being able to trust on him and his desire for revenge had been correct. She paused for a moment before deciding she could now trust him with the next phase of her plan.

She placed the blue folder on her desk. Jim could see an identical folder on her examination couch. He stood nonplussed. Previously, she had turned her back on him when their meeting was over, but on this occasion other hints were being generated. He sat down as he wondered what was about to happen next. The question forming ponderously in his mind was answered sooner than he'd realised.

Suddenly, elegantly manicured hands with crisp acrylic nails lifted her skirt, tantalisingly at first for the tight pencil skirt resisted such direction of movement. She carefully inched the skirt ever higher as Jim's mouth opened with shock and awe. He felt his collar tightening, for one thing. After what seemed like an age, taught, muscular thighs were uncovered as she sought the lacy top of one of her hold-up stockings. She slipped the stocking slowly from her thigh and down her leg with the level of care Cleopatra might have shown when rising from a bath of pure milk. She held up the stocking to the light and reached for a bottle of perfume on her desk, spraying it carefully before slipping it into a large freezer bag, which was also on her desk. Only then did she turn as her skirt was coaxed back to assume its normal position.

Jim's mouth remained open, his dark weasel-like eyes staring intently.

She looked at him challengingly. 'Take this.'

His mouth closed as words formed. 'Aren't you gonna take the other one off?' he suggested, his face flushed and the collar around his neck now seeming to tighten even more. His voice continued to tremble with anticipation.

'No, you disgusting little man,' and then as she realised she still needed him. Her face softened into a smile for just a moment, as she understood he had one more task to perform for her. 'You only get the other one if you do exactly as I say.'

Jim nodded, a slight pant now given off by his crackly lungs as he did so, accepting the polythene bag and also her next instructions. Only the flickering of his left eyebrow betrayed his sense of surprise.

Within minutes he was departing once again. Rita gave a little shiver, washing her hands thoroughly, while her brain had trouble erasing the distasteful image of the ex-reporter. She recognised that her momentary discomfort was well worth the price, given his usefulness to her cause. How easily men could be manipulated— even that poor example of manhood. Once more, a smile decorated her face.

Chapter VII

Formal Complaint

Rita could barely restrain herself: the trap was sprung and her prey was about to be brought down. She wasn't looking for a swift honourable kill but a lingering, painful demise. How she managed to wait until the following day she would never know. Excitement coursed through her brain until well into the small hours. Her active mind completely denied her any sleep at all. She reasoned that this was a small price to pay: she knew that she was now ready. Escape was also very unlikely. Eventually, she decided to make an early start, arriving at the surgery early enough to make those on the first shift thankful that her presence at that time of day was unusual.

Several blank appointments had appeared in her schedule as patients, upon learning who they were waiting to see, had begged to be booked with other doctors. Only the daft, the destitute, the desperate and the particularly thick-skinned were prepared to see her.

Patience had never been a notable attribute of hers. On this day, however, the game plan she could visualise in her mind's eye dictated that the destruction she was about to unleash had been brought about much more easily than she'd hoped. Now, she only had to hold her nerve. Nevertheless, she'd had some initial doubts about the dishevelled and distasteful ex-reporter, but at last acknowledged that his contribution had been nothing less than essential. Perhaps she would let him have the other stocking after all, although she shuddered at the thought of the grimy man getting his cracked skin and filthy nails on anything so personal— especially as she now had no further use for him.

She continued to wait until her morning surgery had finished. The last patient, a young mother stressing over her baby, had been told to pull herself together and stop disturbing the NHS with what was, without doubt, pure trivia and a waste of everyone's time. As soon as the tearful young woman departed, Rita knew that the time had come to activate the trap that now lay in wait. She grabbed the phone and excitedly tapped the number of the Primary Care Trust, the remnants of which still policed the local GPs and dental services. She asked, politely to be put through to the complaints officer, the strange words being issued with the greatest of determination. As the phone was answered, she did her best to form words that she hoped a concerned young woman might use, rather than the more typical strident tones she employed.

'Hello, is that the complaints officer? May I speak with the complaints officer, please?' Her mouth contorted briefly around the unfamiliar polite words she imagined a dippy young woman might employ.

'Yes, my name is Foster. How may I help you today?'

'Hello, yes, well, I am so sorry to trouble you with this. I didn't know where else to turn. I didn't want to give my name but I do want to report something disturbing that I've seen in my GP's surgery and I don't think it's right. I don't really know where to begin.'

William Foster had received several phone calls that morning from disgruntled patients. Most reported GPs leaving patients waiting or receptionists who had not given them an appointment, amongst other typical minor complaints that he habitually received. He dutifully recorded them all but knew full well that they were hardly the sort of thing that he was retained to investigate. He looked down the list of complaints that he'd received since arriving at his office at 9am. There was nothing there to get his teeth into, and he assumed that this histrionic young woman was unlikely to offer anything remotely interesting. He stifled a yawn as he reached for his pad and pen: the boredom rising to a stupefying crescendo within.

'If you could give me some details, Miss?' He went through the form of words he seemed to repeat with every phone call he'd taken. He wondered if anyone believed them or if they were aware that they were automatically trotted out.

'As you may know, I am the PCT complaints officer and I am employed to record and investigate complaints that any NHS stakeholder—'

'You mean *patient*,' she interrupted, almost scoffing down the handset.

'Yes, precisely that,' he offered as he desperately looked for his place on the pre-printed card from which he was reading.

'That any NHS, ah, *patient*, may wish to make with regard to the service they have received from their GP or dentist. You may also know that the PCT has an obligation to investigate each complaint that we receive, and if such complaints cannot be resolved locally, we then are empowered to notify the General Medical or General Dental Council.'

Rita was now thoroughly bored by the droning voice of the stupid man. She grew impatient to move things on. Her agile mind took control of the conversation. 'I was really shocked and upset by what I saw. I know it just isn't right,' she managed a sniff, as if she was choking back a tear.

Mr Foster sensed something unusual and abandoned the words he was planning to continue to convey from the laminated card that he kept on his desk by the phone.

'Are you able to tell me just what you saw?'

The GP smiled to herself, recognising that she was now in control of the proceedings. She fashioned another little sob, thereby raising his curiosity still further. 'Well, I was so shocked. I've never seen anything like it in my life. I thought my GP was such a good man, and then I saw him do this.'

Mr Foster swallowed very hard. His eyes widened and his palms moistened a little as a fine tremor of anticipation now set in. He'd been waiting all his career for something juicy, worthy of the sharp teeth he had been given, but never had been able to use—until that moment, he dared hope. 'Please just take your time, madam, and tell me as soon as you feel able,' he coaxed, struggling to keep excitement out of his voice. How he wished for the bored unmoved tones that he displayed of just a few moments before.

Foster pressed the record button on his phone, sensing that his moment had come. He could already detect the makings of a case worthy of his talents, and his station.

'I went in to my GP's consulting room. It was horrible. I didn't think I would see that.'

'And just what did you see?'

Rita, so used to controlling others, bending and shaping, especially men, to her will, was now in the driving seat. She knew a little tantalisation was needed at that point. 'I am so upset. I don't think a GP should behave that way. I've read in the papers of course but I never thought I'd see it first-hand. I am not sure I can bring myself to tell you. Perhaps if I phone back?'

'Please calm yourself, madam. I am here to help you. Can you elaborate on just what you've seen?'

'No, it's too terrible, the bastard.'

'Pardon?'

'I said, it all happened so fast.'

'Oh, please do carry on. I have a feeling I will need to hear what you are about to tell me.'

'You'd better, you dozy twit.'

'Pardon?'

'I said, I s'pose, I should get on with it.'

'Yes, please, madam, please do continue.' He looked at the little light, recording what he now knew was to be of absolutely momentous significance. This, he knew, was a career-making discovery.

'I got to the GP's room. His door was ajar so I tapped and went in. He was… I am not sure I can say any more.'

'Please do go on, Miss, or others may go through what you have suffered.'

He hoped that appealing to her sense of duty would be enough to get her to complete her story. His anticipation and excitement were now rising in tandem.

'He was actually sniffing some white powder on a metal tray on his desk.'

Christmas had come early that day for Mr Foster. His department had been threatened with cuts. Now he knew this would be definitely placed on hold. Here job-security, perhaps even fame and promotion—and all in one slightly tearful telephone call.

The distressed female continued. 'He seemed really surprised to see me, made some excuse about having a cold and placed a little packet of the white powder in his bottom-right desk drawer.'

'You say the bottom-right desk drawer?'

'Yes, I am sorry. I was so upset. I *think* it was that drawer.' Rita paused to take a bite of a nice custard-filled doughnut she'd brought from the staff room. It made her voice sound even more hesitant and nasal as she sat back in her chair, putting her feet on her desk. 'He thinks I'm stupid. I know what cocaine is. Well, I mean, you know what I mean. What else could it have been? I was shocked, upset and afraid. I turned to go. Then he had a glassy, fazed look about him and asked me what I wanted. He seemed so angry. I made some excuse I was too upset. I couldn't see any more. It was just too horrible. He's always been so nice but never did I suspect this. His life has changed so much. It must be his new lifestyle I guess.'

'So, what do you think was going on, madam?'

'Well, cocaine of course.' Rita had to check herself at this point as she fought down the urge to scream down the phone 'you stupid man!' But she did manage a sniff as she chewed a little more of the doughnut.

A long pause then took place. Mr Foster was receiving the thanks and accolades that were about to come his way. He always knew that he was destined for greater things, and surely the Chief Executive role would now be within his grasp.

'Ahem. Miss, can you tell me who your GP is?'

'Yes, uh I mean, no. I mean, will he get into a lot of trouble?' Rita had now stood after polishing off the doughnut that she had pinched from a receptionist without her knowing. She looked at herself in the mirror: her reflection nodded its head vigorously back at her as a wicked smile flooded across her face.

'I realise this is painful for you, miss, but of course we now have a duty to protect other patients, and it sounds as though we'll need to complete a full and far-ranging investigation. If your report is correct, we have a duty to investigate and to protect vulnerable patients.'

Rita was now swaggering round her room as if she could hear a waltz of pure joy. A receptionist who thought that she had departed on her visits unwittingly barged into her room. Rita covered the mouthpiece and shouted. 'Get out, bitch, now!'

'Pardon?' came from Mr Foster.

'Oh, I said, I feel like a witch.'

'No, not at all. Are you able to tell me the name of your GP?'

'It doesn't feel right.'

'Miss, his name, *please*,' the last emphasis more pleading than exhortation.

'Well, if you must know?'

'I must. I *implore* you. Let me do my job.'

'Matt Sinclair'

'Matt Sinclair?'

Rita was now jumping up and down with excitement.

The pause as Foster now digested this information was enough to stop moons in orbit around Jupiter. 'You did say, Matt Sinclair?' Mr Foster confirmed.

'Yes. I'm so sorry but I have to tell you what I saw.' Another sob was delivered down the phone line whilst Mr Foster's head started swimming.

Rita sat down carefully, her long legs placed once again on her desk as she reclined in her sumptuous leather chair.

'You mean *the* Matt Sinclair?'

'Yes, I do.' She stifled another urge to complete the sentence with 'you fool'.

Mr Foster had been reeled in, and was, by now, well in the keep-net. Rita delivered the coup-de-grâce. 'He's always been so kind to me. I knew marrying that pop star was going to upset the applecart.'

'Perhaps you are right, Miss.'

'You must think me awful. I suppose he's too big to challenge in this way?'

Mr Foster licked his lips; he could already taste the sweetness that came with rapid advancement. 'No, not at all, nobody can behave in this way and expect to get away with it. We will make urgent and far-reaching investigations.'

He stood in front of the mirror as he adjusted his fringe. He wondered how success and promotion would sit with his long-term girlfriend, who he'd been asking to marry for two years. 'Now, Miss, we will handle it all from here. You must realise these are serious allegations which, if proven, could well end up in suspension or a criminal prosecution.'

'Well, I don't want to get anyone in trouble, but this isn't right, is it?'

'You are quite correct. Are you prepared to give me your name so that we can keep you informed?'

'No, not at the moment. I don't want to be identified. I'd rather not be involved if it's unpleasant.'

'Very well then, Miss. You can always telephone me on this number at any time. Thank you for calling once again, and we will do whatever it takes to get to the bottom of all this.'

Rita replaced the handset. 'I certainly hope so, Mr Foster,' she said to herself, the self-satisfied grin subsuming every other emotion now visiting her face.

She knew that it would take more than one blow to bring him down; this was just a ranging shot, having already prepared the salvo that she knew would blow him out of the water. She picked up the phone in order to make ready the much more momentous shock for the smug and irritating GP. She would have to show him just what it was like to be brought down a peg or two, and if in so doing it destroyed him and that puerile bimbo he'd just married, this was the price to be paid for allowing oneself to become exposed to the heat in the kitchen.

Rita knew it was going to get a lot hotter for the two of them.

Chapter VIII

Single Strand of Bravery

Janice had brought Greg a cup of black but lukewarm coffee, just the way he liked it. They were out of his favourite biscuits so, as she'd finished the photos of the surgery that she needed for her new website, she'd popped out to the local shop in her lunch hour to get some for him. She placed the coffee and plate on his desk and moved much closer, her thoughts surging. She'd never been so happy, and from the moment she'd set eyes upon him, she knew he was the one. Now knowing, without doubt, that he felt the same way magnified those feelings: surely, this was destiny— and destiny couldn't be denied.

His words exploded like landmines going off as she closed the gap between them. 'Janice, I need to apologise to you. We shouldn't have done what we did.'

Even as his words crossed the ether, Janice knew, as if suddenly gifted prescient vision, that her life and her dreams had been built on shifting sand with a brisk tide heading for the beach. She stopped moving towards him. Her brain couldn't handle what she'd just heard and sanction movement at the same time. She summoned, somehow, a single strand of bravery from her world that was about to implode. 'Do you mean we shouldn't have made love or fallen in love?'

'Both,' came the devastating reply, causing the most violent explosion of all to go off as she stopped, her legs quivering but seemingly frozen to the spot.

How she wanted to hold him so that his words would melt, and he would tell her that it was a silly joke and that the words he'd whispered until deep in the night were the ones that mattered, not these.

She looked at him. Clear green eyes stared wide as her heart seemed to shatter into a million tiny shards that would never come together as a whole ever again.

'We two can never be together, Janice. I'm so sorry.'

She remembered the night that they'd shared; the way she'd clung to him and wept in the ecstasy of true love that she knew they both experienced. How could feelings have changed so quickly? She knew she had to know: to understand the things that had destroyed her, her hopes, her dreams and her happiness within a few short days.

'Why is that, Greg?'

'Because I'll be expected to marry my own kind.'

'Who said anything about marriage? And what's *your own kind*? Another man?'

'Don't be obtuse, Janice. I mean someone who is black, like me.'

'Forgive me, Greg, but are these lines from an old play of fifty or so years ago that you've just found and you're now rehearsing?' Janice's eyes stared wider: she couldn't believe what she was hearing. Surely this could only be a poorly presented joke of some kind, and he was about to sweep her up in his strong arms. Nevertheless, his expression and his eyes held the truth that now terrified her. She knew in that moment that she couldn't respond.

71

'Janice,' he began, but could find no more words that would carry through the distressing scene.

Her tormented thoughts then produced more words.

'Excuse me, Greg, but what's your skin colour got to do with our relationship? It isn't a problem for me, my friends or my family. Is it a problem for yours?'

Suddenly, the pause communicated more than any words could.

Eventually, after the most brutal of delays, he found words. 'All my life I've been singled out because I'm black. I know who I am now, and I don't want mixed messages for my kids.' His unfortunate choice of words was not lost on the receptionist.

'That has nothing to do with us, you and me, the love we have for each other. And besides, any children we'd have together would be beautiful.'

'People would look on them as an abomination—neither black nor white.'

She wanted to stop and stare as if she'd not just heard those words. Knowing that a pause would be fatal, however, she continued. 'The boys would have your lovely skin, your muscular build; the girls my looks and eyes. Those same eyes you remarked on not more than a few days ago.'

Greg had other demons to unleash: forces that would overwhelm her demure logic. 'When I was six, I was playing outside a woman's house with my little car. My mum had told me I could run up to the top of the street where the pavement was smooth. The lady rushed out very angry, shouting at me at the top of her voice, asking me what I was doing, asking where was I from. I told her that I lived just down the road. She then got really angry, told me never ever to play outside her house, that she didn't want people of *my sort* to play in her neighbourhood, that I

72

was to go home and never return. I ran home, forgetting the toy car my mum had just bought for me. I knew that I couldn't tell my mum because she would have gone up there and ripped her head off. I knew that if I told my dad he would be upset and be very quiet.' Greg remembered, all too painfully, his dad's rants about people who'd treated and judged him harshly, simply by making assumptions to do with his skin colour. They, according to his father, had failed to see him as a person, and one's character had nothing at all to do with one's skin. The saddest thing of all, however, was that, in recalling this, Greg was about to do exactly the same thing to Janice.

Angels fell from the heavens in that moment, weeping alongside this brave young woman who realised only that she had to keep talking, knowing that this would be their last conversation. 'Greg, that must have been a long, long time ago. People are keen to see a person and his qualities—not his colour. Besides, half the film stars, singers and American presidents are mixed-race, not black.'

Anger conflated with his denial. His deep velvety voice took on a more insistent tone.

'Janice, that's nonsense, they are *black*—like me—and I'll be expected to raise kids just like me.'

'No, it's the truth, and they are clever, intelligent and beautiful. That is precisely why we see so many people of mixed race and black skin on the telly.'

'I don't want that for my kids.'

One desperate question just had to be asked. As her vision misted and her head filled with the destruction of bright thoughts now destined to be replaced with misery, the words flowed from her mouth. 'Do you love me, Greg, like you told me through that night as you wept in my arms, and as I told you that I'd always loved you?'

'Of course. You know I do.' The strained words, the pauses and the most brutal of gaps opened once again, finally giving the lie to the words.

'I'm sorry, Greg, believe me I am so sorry, for a million reasons, and more. I'm sorry.' She fled from the room. Anger and confusion kept the tears away, for now, but she knew this was a temporary reprieve. There began a desperate rush to say all that she had to say, make the request that she now saw as being crucial before emotion disabled her completely. Returning hurriedly to the office, not even Mrs Simpson could miss the heartbreak and distress irreversibly etched across the young woman's face; one that was normally so bright, happy and vibrant.

'Janice whatever's the matter?'

A moment of clarity entered the older woman's mind: she moved quickly to close the office door. Pretty green eyes filled like rivers, bursting their banks, before words could be issued. All the manager could do was hold the poor girl as tears came to claim her, subsuming totally the strength that she'd somehow found moments before.

One request was now so vital that it was made even through the sobbing that formed convulsively, as a deluge of pain hit her in wave after wave.

'Mrs Simpson, could I take some leave? I need to get away. *Please*,' her suffering acute, her words rushed and her torment palpable.

Mrs Simpson knew that things were at a crucial stage with the new extension and that Janice had learned more than most about the new systems that had been set up. She recognised also that the young receptionist was desperately needed: no one knew as much

74

as she. Allowing her to leave so suddenly would spell disaster. Janice had volunteered for so much overtime and extra shifts.

It was in that moment, however, seeing the young woman and her suffering that her boss was reminded of precisely why she had volunteered in such a fashion. Ultimately, her need to get away now, so urgently, was for exactly one and the same reason.

The pause allowed the sympathetic and understanding look to form on her face. To her credit, a kind-hearted nod formed almost immediately.

Janice's discomfort intensified under the look of concern from her boss; somehow, she managed more words. 'If you can spare me, then I can go with my mum and dad to Italy for three weeks. They are leaving tomorrow.'

'Yes, of course, Janice. Off you go.' When all was said and done, even Mrs Simpson knew that only these simple words would serve, given the abject distress that was emanating from the habitually bright and cheerful receptionist.

Tears once again reigned over everything in that moment: the young woman was beset by confusion and disappointment. Shattered dreams lay at her feet, along with a broken heart. How foolish she had been. She managed to hug her boss. She swept a few personal effects in her drawer and departed with no other words being said.

That same afternoon, Rita was meeting with Gaby Smith from Eltraset Pharma.

'It's so good of you to see me at such short notice, Doctor Letworth. You have all been taking part in the study for so long. I can't believe it's finally come to an end. Are these the last of the patient records for those who have been enrolled in the study?' She pointed at a file in Rita's hands. 'It has been so busy. So many GPs have signed up to take part in our South Manchester Acute Respiratory Therapy Study.'

'Well, I cannot deny the financial inducements to get people in the study have been a big boost,' Rita said drily.

'Yes, I suppose so. Nine-hundred pounds a patient is certainly no small reward. Some GPs have recruited a hundred patients.'

'I don't think we are far off that number, Gaby,' Rita said, handing over the large blue zipped file.

Gaby checked the seal.

'Just checking that the secure tabs have been removed. We are not allowed to take them unless the GP has sealed them personally. You know the MHRA is very clear about such things. I could lose my job if I don't make these checks. We have strict rules as to which files we are allowed to accept.'

'Yes, I suppose with so much money being involved we have to stick to the rules.'

'Well, we know there won't be any problem here at Parkvale. That's why we enjoy having you in our studies.'

'Likewise. Have you many more to collect?' Rita asked expectantly.

'No, yours is the last. Oh no, actually, Doctor Sinclair is my last collection. I am over there next.' Her eyes lit up. 'Ooh that hunky Sinclair. I suppose it's only right somehow that he's married one of the most gorgeous women on the planet.'

Rita agreed, her words syrupy, 'Yes, of course. He is *so* handsome.' She exaggerated the words enthusiastically but for too long, causing Gaby to pause for a moment.

'Yes, yes, of course, you are right. I can't believe how things have changed for him.'

76

'Oh, yes, they will be changing for him,' confirmed Rita.

'Sorry?'

'Yes, I said it's a chance of a lifetime.'

Gaby paused for a moment as she digested the words. 'Well, I'd better be off then. Thanks so much, and of course as soon as we've checked the records we'll send you your final cheque.'

'Oh, no hurry for that,' Rita waved her hand casually. Money was the last thing on her mind, which was now running with a much more potent currency.

'Okay then, Doctor Letworth, many thanks.'

Once again, Rita sat back in her chair, her long legs and beautiful shoes resting on her desk. She smiled to herself: she knew this would be the last day of Matt's life as he knew it.

Half an hour later, Gaby was entering Matt's surgery.

'So nice to see you, Doctor Sinclair. As you know, it's the final day of the SMART study. Have you got your final folders?'

'Yes, here are our final two.'

'Oh, many thanks, and thank you for taking part. You seem to have enrolled more than anyone else, so well-done!'

Matt handed over the two zipped folders. 'Oh, just a minute, I think that one needs sealing. Oh, it's done. Doctor Stevens must have sealed it.'

'Okay then, no problem, as long as it's sealed before I remove it. Many thanks, Doctor Sinclair. So nice to see you again, and thank you again for taking part.'

'No, Gaby, thank you for approaching us. We have really enjoyed taking part. It's been a bit of a rush with everything that's been happening, but hopefully we have some good patients recruited.'

'Oh, I am sure you have. Righto then, Doctor Sinclair, I'd better go and let you get on with your surgery.' She paused just for a moment, bright eyes staring at him, before departing with only a single glance.

That night, Matt had another visitor, although this person stopped short of approaching the house, preferring to confine his attention to Matt's car, which, as usual, was left unlocked. Footsteps were made with infinite care: the loose gravel insisted on making a tell-tale crunching noise as weight was shifted over its surface. Having accomplished his task, the shadowy figured departed in seconds with a self-satisfied smile: he knew it would be soon time for him to retain his old job, and his pariah status would soon come to end.

Chapter IX

Possession

The following day, Matt started his surgery as usual. As it was drawing to a close, Millicent, one of the new receptionists, came down to his room. Her voice was trembling with nervousness as she conveyed that a Mr Foster was waiting for him from the PCT, along with two police officers. Matt knew that William Foster was the complaints officer. He had first-hand, but mercifully little, contact with him. An enquiry from him always involved lots and lots of reports to write and an even greater number of forms to fill in, before he was satisfied—and that was with the minor stuff.

Matt saw the last patient and then immediately went into the waiting room.

'My goodness! Mr Foster, officers, why so serious?'

Mr Foster chose not to look directly at Matt. He was here to do a job and not get charmed by pleasant chitchat. He also didn't want his eyes betraying the sense of opportunity that he could now feel coursing through his veins: the opportunity this stupid and decadent GP had gifted him.

'Actually, Doctor Sinclair,' he began.

'Please call me Matt,' the GP offered pleasantly, but the words died a lonely death on the distance opening steadily between the men. Matt's head was now wheeling with anxiety and fear. Later, he could neither remember leading the men into his consulting room, nor offering them coffee.

'To come straight to the point, Doctor Sinclair, we have received a highly disturbing allegation about you.' The smile flickered in the corner of his mouth, despite valiant attempts by the manager to suppress it.

'About me?' Matt voiced, shock resonating in his voice. He sat down, the three grave faces fixed upon him in much the same way a Republican official might look at one of the few remaining French aristocrats waiting for 'La Guillotine' to be reset to its highest position.

'Well, please, let's hear it. Have I done something wrong?'

Matt couldn't understand why the police were in attendance. A patient complaint would never be handled in this way, and only then if there had been a serious incident like a suspicious death.

'We have a report that you have been seen snorting a white powder between patient appointments. Presumably cocaine.' Mr Foster looked very carefully at the GP to see if his facial expression changed from sheer puzzlement or if there was now any hint of guilt appearing.

'I see. You mean someone has reported having seen me do this?' Matt's facial features remained calm, though he could feel a sickening thud in his stomach and his pulse rise.

Matt couldn't understand why this should happen now: his patients were generally very loyal, and he seemed to get on with them all very well. He reasoned that this could only be some sort of grudge allegation, but could not think of anyone who could have been upset in this way.

'We are not at liberty to mention the accuser,' Mr Foster declared pre-emptively.

'Why am I not surprised,' Matt could only think to himself.

'We were told that upon snor—, umm, *taking* the white powder in this way,' Mr Foster continued, 'a small packet was replaced in your drawer.' Mr Foster paused between sentences as if reading a long list of accusations against a condemned man. 'Would you mind if we take a look?'

Matt knew they could not insist—even with the police present. He also knew that he had nothing to hide. 'Please, be my guest,' he said, indicating towards the seven drawers in his desk. Mr Foster opened the bottom right drawer as if he knew exactly what he was going to find and where he was going to find it.

The police officers had neither moved nor said anything throughout the whole encounter. One moved suddenly as if a switch had been thrown. Leaning forwards he moved to hold him back, producing a pair of tweezers, plastic gloves and a sealable specimen bag. He delicately removed the bag containing the powder from the drawer, using the tweezers to shake it, and sniffed carefully before sealing it in the evidence bag.

'I must warn you that if this does test for cocaine, this is a Schedule A drug,' the policeman offered clearly and slowly.

Shock enveloped Matt: he knew in that tiny fragment of time the sample had been placed there deliberately—but by whom and why. Moreover, who would want to harm him in this way? His heart was now racing so much that he knew his outward appearance could no longer contain the changes it was producing in turn.

Mr Foster saw the look of fear appear fleetingly over Matt's expression, it was soon to be joined by other, more painful emotions. He licked his lips like a hungry man at the appearance of a feast. 'We will test the contents, and of course take a signed statement from the witness,' came from Mr Foster, in his eagerness to speak before the policeman.

'Can you tell me who your witness is?' Matt asked desperately.

'No, of course not,' Mr Foster offered with an almost aggressive disdain.

'Okay then, can you tell me *when* I am supposed to have snorted this substance?'

Mr Foster now became a little more vague. 'We will have a full statement soon, and then we'll be back for you, Doctor Sinclair,' he said perfunctorily.

Bill Foster knew that here was his moment: he recognised that sorting this issue quickly and boldly would be bad for the GP but good for himself. The public would pounce on this story like a cheetah outrunning its prey—and they would demand the action that would follow. Surely, if this also led to his advancement, then no one could possibly object. The GP only had himself to blame. He detested people who thought that perfectly good rules did not apply to themselves. What a stupid man. He deserved the punishment that would follow. No doubt he now thought of himself as some sort of celebrity and not an ordinary chap. Well, he was about to find out that plain and ordinary rules, such as the force of the law, still applied. These rules, far from bouncing off him, as some thought the cult of celebrity demanded, would destroy him. This, for sure, was one instance where the guilty would receive the punishment due. He would singlehandedly see to it.

Matt went very quiet. To the three witnesses in the room, this could only mean a confirmation of his guilt. Matt acted quickly, all three men seemed stunned by the sudden movement. He tapped three digits on his desk phone.

'Carol, could you pop in for a moment?'

Carol was the Practice Nurse, and within a couple of minutes she had knocked and entered. Shock and surprise vied for prominence on her face as she saw the four of them sitting there, each with very different expressions.

Matt selected two blood bottles from the tray in his stainless steel trolley and also two sealed, sterile sample containers. 'Carol, could you take two samples of blood from my arm?'

'Yes, of course, Doctor Sinclair.'

'What would you like them tested for?'

'Cocaine levels.'

Carol swallowed hard; she could now understand the reason for the tension in the room, as if a storm was about to precipitate from the heavens. Her eyes widened as she looked at her boss. She blinked excessively while trying to retain a professional veneer, but knowing that simple words would help her at this point.

'Yes, of course, Doctor Sinclair.'

Mr Foster looked a bit queasy as the samples were taken. For Matt and Carol, however, their professional instincts of handling unexpected developments were now firmly in force and could be seen on their implacable faces. Matt labelled them and bagged them both. He did this in sight of the three men who sat watching his every move. Whilst thanking Carol, he offered one to Mr Foster and asked her to send the other off to the local hospital for cocaine levels. He plucked a couple of hairs from his scalp and divided them into two, placing equal lengths in each of the sample bottles. 'Send one of these for cocaine levels please, Carol,' whilst offering the identical specimen to Mr Foster.

The policeman spoke as he stretched in front of the PCT official and spoke. 'We will test these for cocaine.'

Possession

Matt knew that, if the story was correct, levels of cocaine would be present either in his blood or in his hair samples, depending on when the alleged incident was supposed to have taken place. The hair samples in particular would allow testing for exposure to cocaine over several weeks, and if negative would be a strong rebuttal of the allegations against him.

At this point, confidence could be seen across Matt's face. Mr Foster looked a little shocked as the queasiness subsided. Matt now knew he had set in motion a train of events that would prove his innocence. His other worry about who would want to do this to him and why refused to quieten.

Carol departed with a mixture of agitation and curiosity. She almost bumped into the doorframe, unable to tear away her eyes from the scene.

'Well, gentleman, you have all you need, and I look forward to hearing from you.' Matt continued to plumb the furthest reaches of his memory for any clues—anything that might reveal who would want to bring him down in this way. He could only consider that this was much more than a joke in poor taste, and that the perpetrator, whoever he or she might be, was intent on doing him serious harm.

Mr Foster and the policemen rose. He knew that a simple act of bravado was not going to deflect him now: he reasoned that most GPs were hardworking, honest and reliable, but that there were one or two rotten apples in the barrel, and these needed to be removed so as to protect the rest. This was precisely what he was retained for.

'We will let you know as soon as we have had the samples tested. If it does prove to be cocaine, you will be suspended pending a full hearing.' Mr Foster did his best to hide the distaste on his face, but the words were almost spat out so as to not leave much doubt about his real feelings.

Matt nodded, knowing that the blood and hair samples would be clear and that such a suspension, if it were applied, would be only temporary. He naively hoped that this would be the end of the matter.

Carol had immediately gone to the office and reported her new-found knowledge to an incredulous but eager practice manager. For once, she could not believe just what she was hearing.

'Cocaine? *Cocaine* did you say?' she queried initially with alarm, then continued, 'Upon my word: you hear about these things amongst these rock stars but I wonder what on earth's come over him?'

'You can't possibly think it's true!' declared Carol sceptically.

'You know these celebrities don't lead normal lives, like us common folk.'

'But, it's our *boss*, and he's *never* put a foot wrong.'

'Any of them, any of these men, can get up to no good. Trust me, I know it's hard-wired inside—mischief,' offered Mrs Simpson with her usual authoritarian style that had now re-exerted itself. 'My first husband, he got up to all sorts while my back was turned, and most of it with the woman over the road. They are all led by their eyes and their noses and other things.' She tapped her own nose as if tipping the wink on information that every woman knew about every man.

'Yes, but Matt's not like that!' Carol offered quickly.

'Trust me, they are *all* like that when they get a bit bored,' the manager assured her.

'You can't surely think...'

Possession

She quietened quickly as the three visitors travelled back through reception. As soon as they'd gone, Carol's shocked tones issued forth once again, but just as she was about to express her disbelief, her boss appeared in reception in order to obtain his prescriptions for signing before departing out on his home visits. The information spread through the small surgery like a gas main going up. Within seconds even the part-time filing clerk had been given the 'exclusive'.

He did his best to appear his normal bright self, but all the girls could tell that much more serious undertones had hampered his habitual jovial manner and were quietly eating away at it. What was more relevant he could tell that each of them knew. Behind each quick glance and forced smile, they were now assessing him, hopefully kindly, but then, of course, one never knew what others really thought. Perhaps this was a good thing.

None could have guessed that there was much worse to follow; this was no more than the lit fuse leading to a much more substantial conflagration. In any event, his mind was incapable of predicting the intensity and the extent of the blast that was about to rip through his life. The unease that he could feel rising within was as nought to what awaited him.

The following day Mr Foster returned with the same policemen who had accompanied him the day before. A stout woman accompanied them, who said very little but who wore a fierce facial expression that neither polite talk nor courtesy could extinguish. Matt wondered mischievously if she had been employed as a security guard in case there was trouble. He didn't have to wait long to find out who she was.

Mr Foster began speaking in something of a rush. He could not quite hide the delight on his face. He had read about these maverick GPs who though they could get away with just about anything. For sure, it was time to demonstrate that the truth was very far removed, and as an added bonus, Mr Foster had been given assurances that his career would soon take a more uplifting pathway as soon as this matter was settled.

'I'm afraid the sample of powder has come back showing that it's cocaine. Detective Williams will need to interview you under caution, and I am afraid I am going to have to suspend you forthwith.'

Matt could tell by the expression on the complaints officer's face that regret was the last thing he was feeling.

'Doctor Gumper is here to begin an indefinite locum, until such time as we have this matter sorted.'

'We are to escort you from the premises as soon as DI Williams has his statement.'

Matt's mind had focused on very little else in the night: he had prepared for this possibility, though his mind still could not think who would wish to plant evidence and harm him in this way.

Dr Gumper announced in a booming voice that she was just going out to her car in order to fetch her medical equipment. She looked at Matt's chair, mentally trying it on for size and with an air of expectation. She'd never been busier: there were so many GPs just like this one who were giving the whole profession a bad name, and as soon as 'Sexy Sinclair' was out of the picture, she could stabilise the practice and get it back on an even footing. She doubted that he would be back, and the PCT would soon act to dismiss him for gross misconduct. Her mind's eye could already see the advertisements that would soon be placed for his successor. She also knew that, as soon as such announcements were made, patients would start drifting away in droves. This was human nature, of course, and had nothing to do with her. She'd always found a direct approach to work best with nearly all patients, and the fact that most practices to which she'd been sent lost half their list was solely to do with people deserting a sinking ship.

Dr Gumper looked round at the no-doubt expensive new building works. It followed, as thunder followed lightning, that once patients started wandering away and signing up at other surgeries, the place would soon be rendered non-viable. Closure would follow swiftly in order to save money, and the staff would lose their jobs. The medical staff, in particular, would be unlikely to ever work again with such a stain appearing on their CVs.

Dr Gumper thought how much she would have liked to have a surgery just like this one. It was a crying shame that the PCT would not let her re-join the Principal list that would allow her to have her own practice once again. She now thought about the events of five years' past, and the pacemaker that had been left in a deceased patient. They said it was her fault, that she should have checked and informed the doctor who signed off the deceased for cremation, and also the undertaker. They said it was her responsibility to make sure that the radioactive device was removed before the patient was cremated. In truth, perhaps a tiny error on her part, but one that they were wrong to blame her for in the way they did. It was only a small explosion, with nobody hurt, although she acknowledged that the crematorium had to be closed for three months as a direct result. In any event, what they did to her was nothing compared with what they'd do to a drug-snorting GP like this one.

Matt knew that the samples would be back in a day or two. 'You have no proof that this sample is mine,' he stated.

'Might I remind you that this is a Class A scheduled drug, and it's been found in your possession,' came from DI Williams.

88

'But surely anyone could have placed that in my drawer.'

'Remember, we have a witness who said that she saw you sniffing white powder and putting it hastily back in the drawer,' advised Mr Foster, brusquely.

'Very well then, in that case, I take it you have dusted it for fingerprints.'

'It's not always possible to demonstrate fingerprints,' concluded the detective.

'Could that be perhaps because there aren't any? And certainly none of mine! Has this witness come forward?' Matt still detected that something wasn't being said.

'She will as soon as you have been suspended and removed from your surgery,' Mr Foster assured him.

'Presumably then this female is a patient of mine who must be registered with me, and if she says she came in to see me, she will be known to the surgery.'

'All in good time, Doctor Sinclair. Once you are removed we can begin the necessary checks,' said Mr Foster, hoping that his face would not now betray the weakness of his position.

'So then, if my samples come back completely negative, as I am fully expecting them to, this would tend to refute your witnesses allegations and, I would suggest, her entire story? Especially, as I suspect, that even *you* do not know who this person is! Does that not strike you as being strange?'

In his haste for advancement, Mr Foster had neglected to carry out the simple checks and balances that would be needed to bring down the GP. He had convinced himself all too easily of his guilt, and this had stood in the way of common sense. He wasn't to be diverted now. He had too much riding on this case, and he needed to make sure it was brought in with himself, in particular, shown in a good light—regardless of how everyone else appeared.

89

Possession

'You are in possession of a class A drug, I would remind you, and we have to take action based on this.'

'Very well then.' Matt rose to go and placed a few personal effects in his briefcase. Mr Foster and the policemen looked carefully as each item was placed in his bag.

Greg Stevens appeared at the door. 'Matt, what's going on?'

'I'm not at all sure, Greg, only that I have been suspended. Mister Foster here has had a tip-off that I was seen snorting coke and placing a little bag in my desk. The sample has tested for cocaine.'

Greg laughed. 'You are joking?'

'I only wish I were. My blood and hair samples should be back in the next few days and I am expecting them to be completely clear.'

Mr Foster coughed a little nervously. He then remembered all those politicians who had called press conferences in order to put forward their case; those who'd shouted their innocence from the rooftops only for them to be prosecuted days later, their lies exposed as a flimsy camouflage for the real truth that they were attempting to cover.

'I wonder then, Mister Foster, if you could get in touch with your source so that she can corroborate her story?'

'I have no doubt that she'll do exactly that,' Mr Foster offered, suddenly trying to place more conviction on his words than he could feel inside. He knew that he couldn't reveal that he'd moved in this way purely on the basis of an anonymous phone call. He realised now that all he could do was hope that she came forward when the story broke, as he knew it was about to— and in a very big way.

Matt was escorted form the building, and DI Williams arranged a date for him to be interviewed under caution. None of the men saw a reporter crouching behind the low dry-stone wall just over the road. His powerful digital camera clicked furiously as he captured various excellent high-quality images.

Jim Duggan punched the air with unabridged delight. He hoped that his images would be highly sought after and would fetch a fortune. He knew that with this wealth would come notoriety of precisely the opposite kind that was about to come the GP's way. Much more than this, it was time to get back his job—and revenge never tasted so good.

Chapter X

Feint Recovery

Matt drove straight home. Fabienne had returned minutes before, and had also made a start on their evening meal. Mercifully, his agitation and worry had destroyed any appetite, and his assurance that he felt he could not eat a thing was, for once, more real than feigned.

Fabienne sat him down and offered him a cup of tea. She sat facing him in the kitchen, sitting on the same stool that he had sat her down on all those weeks ago when he had fussed over her and offered her coffee with cream and lemon meringue pie.

She placed the hot drink in front of him and just waited for him to tell her what was causing such distress and urgency inside. Studying him carefully, somehow he could not quite meet her gaze, and such was the worry accompanied by discomfort now running within her. He looked down at the cup of tea, no words forthcoming.

Eventually, after some coaxing he revealed the true nature of his anguish.

'Matt, who would want to do such a thing? Could it be a joke?'

'No, it's far too serious for that.'

'But who would harbour such a grudge against you?'

She thought of the times when she'd hidden amongst the aisles of the local supermarket or at the cinema. Wherever she had ventured, she'd heard people say nothing but nice things about their wonderful GP, and she knew that his name would appear next in such conversations. The marvellous thing about a disguise was that it not only granted anonymity, but also allowed that person to discover some powerful home truths on a vast variety of subjects.

'Sylvie, I just can't think who would want to do that to me. Let alone why.'

The unknown person who obviously hated him enough to want to hurt him in this way, in many ways weighed more heavily on him than the offence of which he had been accused, but of which he was innocent. Her eyes now at their deepest meditative blue studied him with concern at the thought of this man who lived for his work, for helping his patients, and yes for the adoration that was sometimes seen in their eyes. How different now the circumstances were from those to which he was more accustomed.

'Matt,' she said for the hundredth time, 'someone wants to hurt you. Who could it be?'

'Nobody I can think of,' he replied with honesty.

Suddenly she stood up, as might an excited schoolgirl on learning that Christmas was to be a day early. This was the most compelling thing about bright thoughts: for with them came bright ideas and suggestions. She raced round the worktop, holding out both her hands in order to grab both of his. Her cheerful manner was, as always, irrepressible, but never more so than when skies appeared dark and foreboding.

'Come on Matt, we need a bit of help.'

She led him out onto the drive. Her Audi R8 was still ticking a little as the multicylinder Lamborghini engine cooled in the night air.

The car roared into life, and he just had time to click his seatbelt before he was pushed back against the head restraint, the car accelerating quickly down the road as she flicked the wheel-mounted paddles to change gear. Despite his predicament, he couldn't help but remember her discomfort with the manual gear lever in the blue Beetle she'd hired the night she appeared on his doorstep. Here was the confident and capable woman he'd glimpsed in Salford Quays as she now took charge of the situation.

A few minutes later, the car was brought to a precipitous halt on Steve's drive. The low-slung car was just able to cope with the steep slope that lead to his front door—unlike the high heels she was wearing. Still with that sense of excitement, she nevertheless managed to race round from the driver's exit, tugged him from the passenger door, and then went ahead of him to tap on Steve's door, knowing somehow that the doorbell would still not be working, despite the interval of several weeks since they'd visited.

Steve offered them a seat whilst Mary listened intently before popping into the kitchen.

'Tricky one, this, Matt. Is there anyone, anyone at all, that you've upset of late? It might be something simple like a refusal to give a sick note or support a patient for some benefit.'

Matt laughed, Steve looking a little hurt.

'Don't scoff, Matt. Doctor Rowles over at the Partington surgery was stabbed last week when he refused to provide morphine to a heroin addict.'

'Forgive me, Steve, but these are not my typical patients in Perrilymm. There isn't a lot of drug use about, and most people see a sick note as a punishment!'

'Think, Matt. Someone somewhere is gunning for you, and this is I suspect a highly co-ordinated attack. I agree it's not just some vengeful whim from a disgusted patient, though I know you won't have any of those,' he offered when he saw Matt's hurt look.

Mary returned to the room bringing a tray of tea. Fabienne shot from her seat to help her when she detected the wince of pain as she bent her back. 'Mary, I'm so sorry, let me help you.'

'Now, don't you be going and making an invalid of me, Sylvie. I've had to have the same chat with a certain other person,' she said, looking in Steve's direction. 'I've told him it's a pregnancy, not a climb up Everest.' She straightened and rubbed her back encouragingly.

'Feels like a climb up Everest,' Steve offered

'Pardon?' said Matt

'I said, she feels like a rest,' Steve clarified as Matt reconsidered the words that he could have sworn he'd heard whilst shrugging slightly.

'I can't just sit back and watch you struggle, Mary,' came from Fabienne.

'Now, my dear, it's absolutely no struggle, and I am hoping you'll be a much more frequent visitor here because I've read that you are between concerts for a few weeks? Also, I've not forgotten about the cookery skills we were going to share.'

'Mary, that's so kind. I hope I won't be any trouble, with you being pregnant?'

'No, good heavens, not at all. It's better if I keep myself busy. It's only a baby I'm having, though Steve tells me I'm eating too much.'

'I keep telling her that it's not a baby rhinoceros she's having,' Steve offered hurriedly, 'but a sweet baby,' he added as she shot a cautionary glance in his direction.

'Okay then. Well any day that suits you, I'll be right round.'

'Forgive the interruption, but may I remind you that we are no nearer to finding our secret mole who is intent on mischief for poor Matt here?' Steve clarified.

Some hours later, Matt and Sylvie stood, agreeing it was time to depart. Fabienne reached for her car keys. In that moment, a burst of inspiration alighted on Steve's consciousness, like a most beautiful butterfly. Suddenly, he gazed into the distance, as might a seer on divining the affairs of men. 'Sheila Coombs!' he said as the clarifying bolt drove away the obscuring fog that had hitherto beset them all.

'Sheila Coombs!' Matt repeated.

'Yes, indeed, Matt,' Steve continued. 'The last time you saw her, if I am not mistaken, you were snatching a petrol bomb from her grasp at the MEN Arena!'

'Yes, Steve, just before she was about to drop it on me!' Fabienne confirmed with a shudder, recalling the close shave she'd experienced that night.

Mary kissed her husband; barely concealed pride and admiration shone in her eyes as she looked at him.

'Was she not locked up?' queried Matt.

'Briefly, Matt—and all too briefly, some of us would offer. Apparently she agreed to go back on treatment, regretted what she had done and was then promptly released to the care of Professor Harrison.'

'So that means we're all in danger if we are to rely on that man.' Matt opined with more discomfort than anger.

'As you'll recall, Matt, she is clever, resourceful, and it might well be that she still bears a grudge against the man who foiled her attack.'

'Do you think that our friend Professor Harrison can be prevailed upon to release some details about his patient?' Matt asked.

'I do believe so, my boy. If I telephone him tomorrow he may just be persuaded, colleague to colleague, and all that, to give us more information—and especially as regards her whereabouts.'

'Many thanks, Steve. And if you'd let me know as soon as you have spoken to him, I'd be grateful.'

'Yes, yes of course, Matt. I'll telephone you as soon as I have spoken with him and we'll see what he knows.'

'Sylvie, it's been lovely to see you again. I'm free all week if you would like to get together for exchange of cooking ideas. Baby permitting,' Mary offered, patting her tight abdomen.

'Mary, I'd love that. Many thanks.'

Fabienne clung to Matt, her heels not coping with the slope that fell away steeply, as they said their goodbyes and went to find her car.

The following day, Matt was doing his best to occupy his mind, sitting in the conservatory, trying to read the newspaper. He'd walked down to the local newsagent and, although he did not take the *Daily Scorcher*, he could see that he'd made front-page news. Pete Timms, the newsagent, had clearly been discussing events with one or two customers: a deathly silence descended as soon as Matt appeared, and embarrassment arose in shades of pink on the faces of those present. Matt selected his newspaper and handed over his money. He pointed to the *Daily Scorcher* that was on the top of a rapidly diminishing pile, and did his best to acknowledge their inevitable interest in the story.

'Fame at last, eh, Pete,' he offered, doing his best to generate a smile.

Matt had always supported local businesses and Pete's newsagent was no exception. The shopkeeper knew that a great many had taken deliveries from one of the nearby mini-supermarkets, simply using him for forgotten last-minute items. He knew about such things as loyalty, friendship and sticking with people through good times and bad.

'Like most storms, Doctor S. It'll pass. Good luck,' he offered.

Matt smiled and nodded, hoping his words would be proven correct sooner rather than later. Before he left, he noted the leading article that had been composed by Jim Duggan, complete with a full-page spread. Copies were clearly selling quickly.

He walked home slowly, his usual fast, bouncy pace now much slower and more plodding. He returned to his favourite room, the conservatory, where uplifting light always seemed to permeate. Doing his best to concentrate on his paper, he gave up the attempt as a futile one when he realised that he'd read the same word five times but could not recall the context in which it had been placed. Fabienne had taken Mary up on her generous offer to share cooking skills. Matt, with no hint of, shame could only hope that this would be a one-way transfer from Mary, who had always been an excellent cook. He was grateful when the phone rang and he jumped towards it in eager anticipation of some news.

'Hi, Matt. Steve here. I've had a word with your friend Professor Harrison. He doubts that Sheila is involved.'

'Why does that not reassure me?' Matt concluded as he recalled the number of times his mismanagement of his patients had placed Fabienne in extreme danger. He wondered if he was to be the next victim of the psychiatrist's negligence.

'I thought you'd say that so I pressed him and asked him if Sheila has committed to a regular follow-up—this being a condition of being allowed bail.'

'And?'

'Well, it seems that she has kept all her appointments, has slimmed down, smartened up, takes regular showers, has cut down the cigarettes, and seems contrite.'

Matt remained quiet as he considered the words.

'Anyway, he'll put a few direct questions to Sheila when they meet up next week. He has promised to keep me fully informed, and if she defaults on her appointments, he will inform not only me but also the police.'

'Okay, Steve. Sounds good so far,' Matt agreed, but there was more than a hint of suspicion coursing through his racing brain. 'I suppose we just have to trust him,' Matt confirmed reluctantly.

'Yes, for now, but at least he knows that we will be expecting him to keep a very close eye on her and raise the alarm the moment she defaults.'

'Steve, I suppose that's all we can expect for now. Many thanks. Sylvie is with Mary, and I think she's having a cooking lesson from your dear lady wife.'

'I can't believe a girl who looks like that cannot cook. Surely you exaggerate.'

'Trust me, Steve, we daren't invite you round just yet so be grateful that Mary is heavily pregnant.'

Steve laughed. 'I suppose one girl can't have it all. It's only fair that a few lesser skills had to be shared out to us lesser mortals.'

'I tell you, she is just an ordinary girl, Steve.'

'Yes, you just keep telling yourself that, my boy, or one could go mad being in the same house as her, waking up next to her. Sorry, Matt, I'd better go and get a cold shower.'

'I'm sure you'll be fine when the baby's here,' offered his friend.

'Yes, I know. All those sleepless nights and stinky nappies will soon cool me down!'

'You will love every minute of it, I'm sure.'

'Matt, you say just the right thing.'

'I've had a good teacher, Steve.'

'Right, my boy, I am going, and I'll keep you informed.'

'Many thanks, Steve. Speak to you soon.'

No sooner had Matt pressed the 'end call' button than the phone rang again. He recognised the voice of Mr Foster, and could not help but notice a less confident tone.

'Ah, Mister Foster, thank you for phoning. Any news?'

The complaints officer looked skywards as he tried to summon more tolerance. He hated the smarmy GP, and he'd really been hoping to use this complaint as a springboard on to greatness. 'Yes, well, Doctor Sinclair, it looks as though the samples are back and your blood is clear.' Though his tone was quiet, he was quite unable to mask the disappointment in his voice.

'Oh, well, Mister Foster, it doesn't come as a surprise to me,' Matt couldn't help but interject. However, to his credit, his voice held more tones of relief than of wanting to make the man feel small. In any event, still more questions were burning inside. 'What about the hair samples?' Matt remembered, knowing that these would provide further evidence of his innocence.

'Yes, indeed,' Mr Foster coughed over the words he was loath to convey.

'And they are clear too?' Matt prompted.

'Yes, they are,' Mr Foster offered with even more dejection.

'So this means that I cannot have taken cocaine at any time over the past few weeks and probably longer.' Matt knew that Mr Foster would have checked his facts before telephoning the GP.

'Yes, but we still have the sample found in your desk drawer,' insisted Bill Foster, but he was now on an ebb tide, and Matt was now in the ascendant.

'That sample was not mine, and if you'll consider for a moment that your anonymous witness—the one you have not identified—actually says she saw me snorting a white powder, then it is clear that isn't true. I take it you do have a signed witness statement from your *source*?'

'Our source wishes to remain anonymous. As is her right.'

'Very well, Mister Foster, but surely something about her story does not ring true. Have you considered the possibility that this is a plant and that the allegations are nothing but vexatious, holding no substance whatsoever?' Matt asked, shivering a little having offered the wrong word.

Ultimately, Matt had time neither for the other man's hesitancy nor his discomfort: his aim was only to prove his innocence and get back to work.

'Yes, I suppose you are correct,' Mr Foster admitted reluctantly, realising that he was down a blind alley in the dark, and his last torch battery had just been exhausted.

'So, where do we go from here?'

'We'll have to have an inquiry at the PCT.'

'And in the meantime, can I get back to work?'

'Of course not. We need to clarify matters and have a full discussion.'

'I see, except, Mister Foster, with respect, you don't seem to have a lot to go off. Either I was snorting cocaine or I was not. My absolutely clear samples carried out by an independent lab have confirmed that I was not.'

Fabienne entered and kissed him gently, acknowledging his efforts to restrain his impatience and frustration.

'Surely, Mister Foster, I should be allowed back as you have nothing to go off. In addition, allowing me to return to work will save the PCT a fortune from their hard-pressed coffers.'

Matt hoped that this last argument might be the crucial turning point, for so many things these days came down to money. Surely, it was, as always, the lowest common denominator. He knew that Dr Gumper, acting as locum, would mean high costs for the PCT. As Matt's guilt had not been proven, they could only continue to suspend him on full pay, which would mean that cash would be haemorrhaging briskly.

Mr Foster was now in damage-limitation mode. To have accused a high-profile, famous GP was one thing; to do so without a watertight case was another. And then to commit the PCT to a ruinous expenditure would be an absolute disaster for the PCT officer.

'Very well then, Doctor Sinclair, I suppose as you put it like that then I suppose we withdraw our objection and rescind your suspension. However, if anything else of a disturbing nature crosses my desk, then I am afraid, it will go badly for you.'

Matt did his best to hide the relief and excitement in his voice as he offered a 'Thank you for your clarification, Mister Foster,' in as sincere a voice as surging emotions would permit.

At this point, Matt genuinely believed that he was simply allowing his discredited accuser to salvage some pride. In truth, neither man believed that any further revelations would be received implicating the GP.

Mr Foster did his best to preserve a grave note in his voice, but he sensed a wild goose chase and that the GP was in the clear and would most likely remain so. Even more disturbingly, he sensed that, far from enhancing his chances of promotion, these events would set them back by some margin. Everyone loved Matt Sinclair. His failure to bring him down with one quick coup-de-grâce would inevitably mean that his own standing had been damaged; people would distance themselves and supporters would be particularly thin on the ground.

As Matt set down the phone, having secured an agreement to return to his surgery the following day, he could not have known that his fate was being sealed a hundred miles away in the Milton Keynes offices of Eltraset Pharm therapeutics.

He once again dabbed the 'end call' button and turned to Fabienne. 'Sylvie, it's such good news.' He hugged his wife so enthusiastically that she gasped. Strong arms picked her up bodily as he spun her round the conservatory. The light rain had passed and sunshine arrived to illuminate the couple as he looked into her beautiful eyes, framed by her pretty face. He kissed her.

'Wow, someone's pleased,' she offered as she mirrored his delight.

He then relayed the information that Steve had imparted, further stating that Professor Harrison had promised to question Sheila.

Who could blame them for thinking this must surely be the end of the matter.

If Rita had been present, her delight would have known no bounds. She would take unquantifiable delight from the fact that she had successfully distracted them both, whilst the true plan was armed like a live nuclear warhead, itself now on an unstoppable trajectory.

Chapter XI

Fraud Most Brazen

Carol Benyon, head of the SMART respiratory study, looked incredulously at her colleague. She threw his report on the table as if by doing so she would somehow change its conclusions. She could see, however, that the report would remain the same, no matter how many times it was tossed.

'Dave, are you sure?'

'Look, it's pretty obvious. I don't know how he can have been so brazen. There are ten consent forms supposedly signed by patients, who have been recruited into the study. It's the same signature in the same pen. At least ten—maybe more!'

'Surely not!'

'These entire forms are false, even the lung function readings are the same. Have you ever known ten patients, one after the other, to give the exact same readings? Someone is trying to play us for a fool. Did he think we wouldn't check? Surely he'd know that we would pore over every inch of that data. The joke, however, will be on him. These medics think it's a bit of a game. Oh, let's just fill in a few forms—whoops! Just make that bit up and collect nearly a thousand pounds each time I do it.'

'Surely, no one could be that stupid.'

'Please take a look for yourself, Carol. It would seem that nine-hundred pounds per patient recruited is enough to tempt some GPs into defrauding us. At least ten have been falsified in this way—probably the whole batch! I have copied each of those ten study forms. Look, here they are, you can see, anyone can see, sorry, you know what I mean—they've been falsified. I wonder if they are genuine patients at all or whether they've been made up too!'

'I know that nine-thousand pounds is a lot of money, but surely not worth going to prison for as well as losing one's job; being struck off.'

'That's the least that will happen to him. Silly fool.'

'Tell me, then, who is it?' she said with a sigh that reflected the vicissitudes of fame, fortune and fate that were now in store for the foolish GP who was about to feel the full force not only of his colleagues, of the Pharma company, but also the MHRA—The Medicines and Healthcare Products Regulatory Agency that policed the appropriateness of, and standards applied to, studies in the UK. Their reputation for taking action against those found to be in contravention of their strict standards was legendary for its strictness and thoroughness. Massive multinational companies were terrified of falling foul of them: for multi-million pound studies could be held up, or cancelled completely if the MHRA deemed it to be necessary. Their vigilance as regards the adherence to correct standards was all-encompassing, but as nought to that applied to those who had dared to falsify and defraud, with patient safety at risk, and monetary gain at its heart.

'So, go on. Is it anyone I know?' posed Carol.

'Brace yourself.'

'Go On! Tell me!'

'Matt Sinclair.'

'Matt Sinclair! Silly bastard!' she offered with an unfamiliar expletive, almost choking with shock as she sipped on her tea.

106

'That'll be curtains for him,' she concluded as she considered just what could possess a man who was widely regarded as having it all. She could only think it was rather like the film star caught in Tesco with a tin of salmon under her coat.

She sighed with much regret and resignation. She'd always liked him; even before he was famous. For heaven's sake, *everyone* liked him. Perhaps marrying above his social group had turned his head. Perhaps the unusual life that pop stars and celebrities led had, in some way, turned his brain. In any event, she knew there was no possible defence and he would lose everything—including, most likely, the pretty megastar who, for the moment, was part of that life. She knew, too, that it was now out of her hands: failure to report the facts that she'd just been given would mean that her own position would be forfeited. If it had been up to her, she'd have simply told him to pay back the money and never take part again; however, the MHRA would act in a very different way.

'Okay then, phone the MHRA, and the police will be involved soon enough so we'd better brief them—and, of course, his PCT.'

She knew that things would be taken out of their hands with all the speed of a droplet of quicksilver falling down a glass tube. They now had the obligation to inform the MHRA or they would be also deemed culpable, and the MHRA had the power to close down the whole company if the truth seemed elusive.

The gods themselves had visited Mr Foster in the night. Far from offering their condolences at his miscalculation, they were now offering the plaudits—the laurel leaves that reflected his success.

107

He knew as soon as the young woman had phoned him, as soon as he'd clicked his voice recorder to 'on', that greatness lay in store for him. The phone call he'd received before the end of the working day, the night before, simply confirmed what his instinct told him was now waiting for him. For sure, there'd been a bit of a wobble; the debacle with the cocaine sample and the accuser who'd suddenly disappeared combined to be simply a false start to the main event. Here it was, the coup-de-grâce, and he would be swift rather than merciful. He knew that he was dealing with a dissenter, but there would be the prize of discovering that he was also a criminal. Now he had all the proof he needed. Sweet irrefutable proof that was as watertight as a submarine well before it reached crush-depth.

The tornado that had, for a little while, been raging some way off Matt's coastline was now about to make landfall with devastating consequences. The full weight of its destructive potential was now about to sweep through his life and consume or destroy everything in its path.

Mr Foster had done his best to hide the look of self-satisfied delight from appearing on his face as he had arrived bright and early at Matt's surgery, accompanied, once again, by two police officers.

'Mr Foster, so soon.' Matt offered the simple words that were about measure the end of his happiness.

The GP did his best to retain a light tone in his voice, but something of the delight in Mr Foster's demeanour was now unmistakeable. Real fear rose inside as if he'd been granted prescient vision of the destruction that was about to be visited on him- like a submarine now well below its crush-depth.

'Doctor Sinclair, I have received a complaint from Eltraset Pharm therapeutics about irregularities in a study you have just submitted to them.'

'Irregularities?'

'Yes, they have reason to believe that your records have been falsified. An official complaint has been made to the PCT, and also to the police authorities. The MHRA have notified us of their intention to pursue you with the full force of the law.

It was these last words that brought out the punitive smile on the complaints officer's face. A smile that, in that moment, he could no longer be bothered to restrain: he knew he was dealing with scum—and how he hated scum like this. 'These men are here to interview you under caution at Mirfield Police Station.'

Matt swallowed hard. Fear now gripped him somewhere in the pit of his stomach. He stared just for a moment, recognising that the plant of the cocaine sample was simply a warm-up for the main game of destruction—himself positioned at centre-stage. Suddenly, his mind's eye could visualise a life that was barren and bereft of all the wonderful things—the wonderful wife and friends—it contained—at least for the moment. He knew that she'd have to save herself. All that he'd gone through in order to protect her, to restore her to that pinnacle of fame, would be meaningless if she stayed with him. He'd seen how hard she worked to be the person whose very existence was geared to helping others. He understood this was her life—not the concerts, not the fame, not even the music: this was simply the fuel that powered her need to help those very much less fortunate than she. Leaving would be her only chance of continuing what she'd set out to do; what she tried to do with each breath she took.

He saw all of this in the flicker of that moment; knowing, too, that he'd lose his work, his profession—absolutely everything.

He stared ahead, not focusing: the condemned man brought down at last. He shook his head as if doing his best to try to break the panic that had formed as he refocused on the three men.

One of the police officers stood up. For a moment Matt thought he was going to produce a set of restraints, but mercifully this ignominy was to be spared him. Nevertheless, all the staff and patients saw Matt being led away, flanked by the policemen.

Mr Foster took charge with his loud voice booming through the waiting room. 'I am sorry, ladies and gentlemen, but Doctor Sinclair will be helping us with our enquiries, and we will be appointing a locum as soon as we can to keep the practice open. I am sure that Doctor Stevens will be happy to assist you'

At the moment, Greg appeared. 'Matt, again! I see you have more visitors. What now! I thought the cocaine was settled? Are they here about that?'

'I don't know what's happening. It's to do with the respiratory study.'

'What about it, Matt?'

'I wish I knew. Mister Foster says we have falsified records. Sorry, as the PI, they say *I* have fabricated a batch of forms. It seems I have claimed for twenty patients with falsified records.' Matt knew that, as the PI or principal investigator, he was the person who'd signed responsibility for the study, for its accuracy, and who also bore full responsibility for any inaccuracies.

'But that can't be true…'

'Tell me about it, Greg, but they say they have concrete proof. Forms I submitted have been filled in fraudulently.'

Greg's voice was silenced; only the open mouth remained as words failed and silence reigned, with shock as its only journeyman.

Matt knew that he'd done nothing wrong and neither had Greg. They had taken part and practised at all times honest and reliable methods of recruitment. Patients had been turned away rather than taken on if doubts had arisen. Matt, for the first time, had an inkling of what he was up against, and came to realise that he was at the mercy of a malign person, intent on ruining him at the very least.

Mr Foster was once again in charge, his mouth dried but his appetite and his hunger undimmed.

'I'd be grateful if you two gentlemen did not discuss this matter here as we will want to give much more detail at the police station.'

'We will be interviewing Doctor Sinclair, under caution for conspiracy to commit fraud,' one of the policemen confirmed, prosaically, as if he were talking about the weather.

Once again, however, Mr Foster couldn't quite defeat the smile that appeared on his face, although his efforts to do so transmuted his expression as one that might come from an executioner about to place the black hood on his next subject.

Greg finally recovered. 'Matt, I'll phone Fabienne. She'll know what to do next. Don't worry, Matt, we'll sort this out.'

It was Greg's short, stunned words that appeared to seal Matt's fate. He knew that he was floundering, desperate for a coherent form of words and strategy.

All present were horrified, the whole surgery was as quiet as the Serengeti just before dawn.

Though good news always spread quickly, and people were often genuinely amazed and delighted to hear such things, its rate of

111

dissemination always paled by an order of magnitude when compared with how quickly bad news travelled. By the end of the day, not only had the whole surgery or even the whole village come to hear of recent events, but the whole country.

So many came forward to denounce the rushed nature of the liaison, opining long and loud how international megastars always attracted wrong partners and problems wherever they went, and postulating that, surely, Fabienne was no exception? The poor girl was nothing more than a lightning rod for bad people who did bad things. Those who had endorsed the golden couple now found other words and more convenient assessments. Opinions they had really held all along were somehow crafted and aired for the benefit of the viewers—and with the assurance that they had indeed been in the background all along.

After a long interview, under caution, in the police station, Matt was released pending further enquiries into the nature of the complaint made by Eltraset therapeutics. Advice was also being sought from the MHRA. Nobody would want to pursue things without sampling their views. However, if they decided that there was a case to answer then there would be little refuge for the perpetrator.

Fabienne raced to the police station to meet with Matt, but unfortunately, her attempts to display solidarity only gave more fuel to the flames that were now burning as a contagion amongst a parched forest. The *Daily Scorcher* seemed to be in prime position to photograph the star as she arrived at the police station in Manchester. Moreover, although other newspapers rapidly caught up through the day, it appeared that Jim Duggan and the titles owned by Mervyn Boomer were back with a scoop that others could only marvel at, so quick had been their response, and so detailed their information. The *Daily Scorcher* appeared the

112

following morning with a front-page spread, beating all other newspapers off the mark. The leading article, recognised as a worldwide scoop, had been penned by Jim Duggan, who had been rehired on the back of a story that was now too compelling and too momentous to ignore.

Over the next few days Jim was promoted to Chief Reporter. There was to be no let-up as further revelations were to be unveiled by the *Sunday Scoop* over the weekend, offering further exclusive pictures, with the final twist revealed as a requiem to a once-respected GP whose greed, as always, had brought him down. Though Matt protested his innocence and his desire to clear his name, Jim Duggan was quick to remind his readers that politicians had assured us all of the same sentiments, only for them to be sent down a short time later; their lies, along with their polished rhetoric being exposed as double-dealing and perjury by the cleansing blade of the judicial process, that cut through such hubris, like an incandescent heated wire through polystyrene.

That evening, Matt sat stunned in front of the television: although switched on, his thoughts were elsewhere. Fabienne did her best to reassure to engage and to support, but she could see her husband was stupefied by the depth and efficiency of the deception that had been placed comprehensively across his theretofore smooth progress. What was even worse was the fact that he still had no idea who the person responsible was for mounting such a detailed plan—and, more so, *why* they should want to do such a thing.

Matt knew, deep inside, that this was a terminal event—both for his life and his career. Knowing one's innocence did not, by any means, assure freedom: surely the facts spoke for themselves. Those were his blue bags, sealed and secure, which had been collected by the drug rep; those same bags contained information that had been falsified for the purposes of material gain. It did not matter that he professed his innocence, his insistence that neither such a trifling sum, nor money in general, motivated him. This was fraud, pure and simple: ipso facto, as the legal profession would describe it. He knew that, despite her loyalty to him, despite the fact that she knew he could no more have committed fraud than stand on the surface of the sun that she would have to leave, if only to protect herself, this, now, like a man condemned to die, begged for mercy for his loved ones, was the only way forward.

He knew that the time for such a plea, to her, was fast approaching.

Fabienne popped out to the village to get some provisions. She knew that he would be unable to eat, and that cooking for him would be a wasted effort. She decided, however, to purchase some tasty treats to see if he could be tempted. Upon her return an hour later, having borrowed his car, as she retrieved some shopping bags from the back seat, she noticed a diaphanous piece of material squeezed between the seat cushions. This she carefully withdrew, revealing its true nature.

She walked into the morning room, holding the shimmering stocking for Matt's inspection. Matt looked up at the delicate item, and could not help but notice the brash and cloying, all pervading perfume, it gave off as Fabienne held it up.

'That's not mine,' he offered.

'No, I suspected not,' she returned. 'It's almost certainly too small to be one of yours—I certainly don't think it would fit those long legs of yours.' Clear blue eyes surveyed him carefully; his own eyes returned their steady, unwavering cobalt gaze.

'And of course it's not mine,' she said, sniffing towards it a little disgustedly as the odour assaulted her nostrils. Like so many girls of her generation, Fabienne usually went around bare-legged, and only in the deepest of winter did she sport opaque hosiery to complement the short dresses and skirts she wore at that time.

Jim Duggan could not believe his luck. From the time when nothing seemed to go right—the time when he'd been relieved of his post; the time when he'd been outwitted resoundingly by the couple who were firmly in his cross hairs— now nothing could go wrong. He was waiting in the wooded area, facing Matt's house, just as Fabienne rushed from the building. His powerful camera caught the scene with neither flash nor sound. The picture of Fabienne fleeing the marital home would be the next story to break as his newspaper marked the toff couple's fall from grace. How they would come to regret having the gall to try to best him. His grisly smile appeared in full force as more pictures were captured, his shooting not stopping until Fabienne's car disappeared from view as it swept through the village.

Jane Tomkins had closed her shop, Razzle, a little early. It had been a quiet day with few customers. It seemed that many of the local folk were too stunned and shocked to contemplate a trip to the generous mid-winter sale that she'd launched recently. She was sitting in front of her little television, with a chicken curry on a tray on her lap, when the doorbell rang.

She looked through the front window of her cottage and saw a car that had come to a halt on the road outside. She knew, at once, that she'd seen it somewhere before. Having little knowledge of cars but the one that sat ticking in the tiny space just beyond her white picket fence was now a unique and unforgettable sight in Perrilymm.

115

Jane rushed to the door, now knowing whom she would find there. 'Fabienne!'

'Jane, I am sorry to disturb you, unannounced like this, but I need a little help. I wonder if I could impose on you?'

'Fabienne, of course, please do come in.' She closed the door quickly and conspiratorially behind the rock star's back as her instinct now held that she make certain that her neighbour had not been followed.

'I am so sorry for interrupting your meal in this way.'

'Don't give it a second though Fabi—, Sylvie,' she responded, remembering the name that she had been asked to use at the two women's last meeting. 'It was pretty horrible and I realised I wasn't hungry anyway. Can I make you a cup of tea or get you anything?'

The two women squeezed into the bijou kitchen as the kettle brought water to the boil. Two mugs were found from a cupboard and the tea left to brew for just a short interval of time. Jane used the delay to marshal some of her surging thoughts. As it came about, Fabienne was the first to speak.

'Yes, Jane, I was wondering if I could count on you for a little favour?'

'Of course, Sylvie, just name it.'

This established, Fabienne paused just for a moment before framing her request of the young shopkeeper. Jane used the delay to say what had been on her mind for some time.

'I am sure you know, don't you, Sylvie, that I kick myself every day for letting this man out of my sight. That I would be lying if I said that, in my wildest dreams, I hoped that you'd knock on my door, one day, just like this evening. That you'd tell me that you are leaving and that I can have him. That's a dream that comes to me most nights. You know, don't you, how envious

I am of you having him in your life.' Jane's thoughts continued to surge.

Fabienne opened her mouth, but surprise had circumvented speech. Jane continued.

'I hope you know, too, how pleased I am for you both, and that I believe you have each found someone wonderful. How can petty jealousy or my recurring dreams get in the way of that? So, in short, whatever you need me to do to help you, and to help Matt, I'll do it, whatever that may be.'

'Jane, thank you so much for that.' Fabienne leaned forwards to hug her, which only involved a short distance, given the close confines in which both women stood in the tiny kitchen. Tears appeared in both women's eyes, those vital few seconds now needed for each of them to compose themselves.

Jane led her through into the sitting room. 'You know, of course, that he's incapable of doing all those things they say he's done?'

Her answer came in the form of a smile from the rock star, which only served to increase Jane's curiosity even more.

An hour later, Fabienne left, the Audi R8 remaining in front of the cottage with Jane checking on it to make sure it was still there at regular intervals through the evening until she went to bed.

The following morning, a blue Honda Jazz entered the car park at Parkvale Medical Centre. A black-haired, slim woman vacated the car. She wore an impeccable black skirt-suit that complemented both her and her frame, perfectly. The receptionist had trouble understanding the French woman with the very heavy accent, but redoubled her efforts when she realised that she'd come to see Dr Letworth. She knew, from previous experience, that any delay in processing a new patient would go badly for receptionist and patient alike. A short time later, Francoise Delamer entered Dr Letworth's consulting room.

'Ah, yes, Miss Delamer. I see here on your new patient form that you are an ex-patient of Doctor Sinclair?'

'Yes, *Docteur*. I did not like ze events of ze past fuw dayz. I was shocked to zee zuch zings, I can tell yu.'

Rita looked at the young woman with the bob of impossibly black hair that shone in the overhead lighting as she shook her head with a mixture of disbelief and disgust. Her brown eyes blinked back against the intense scrutiny to which Dr Letworth was subjecting the young woman.

'Have we met before?'

'*Non*, I zinc not Madame, Docteur. I wuld av remembered I zinc.'

Rita shook her head as if dismissing her own enquiry as irrelevant. Deep-green eyes, however, continued to bore into those of brown that shone like conkers on an autumn afternoon.

'Well, he's always been a bad one, that Doctor Sinclair, and I think he has finally got his comeuppance. I knew there would be more as soon as they discovered cocaine in his bottom-right desk drawer.'

'Oh, mi gudness I did not know about zuch zings as zat! The embezz, the embe, the fraude was bad enuff. I could not stay in zuch a place,' concluded Miss Delamer.

'Well, let me say right now, you are one of many who have deserted what remains of his practice. I think it unlikely he will ever return, and most likely his next move will be behind bars.

Even if he should return, which I doubt, he'll have few patients remaining.'

The young Frenchwoman's eyes widened, as might a tawny owl's on swooping over moonlit meadows, but more with shock than expectation, while she realised that the doctor was most likely correct, barring a miracle.

She pulled her suit skirt down a little as she got up and picked a single blonde hair from her black opaque tights and, much to Doctor Letworth's annoyance, let it fall to the floor.

The young patient left with her new prescription for the pill and departed. Upon entering the car park, she noted a battered hulk of a car, with rust vying with dirt and faded paintwork to cover the bodywork. Jim Duggan vacated the car as the driver's door was slammed with a shriek of metal on metal, and somehow the rusting locks engaged as he hurried inside, after stubbing out a reeking cigarette and spitting out copious amounts of spittle in the general direction of the young woman. She looked concernedly down at her new black patent shoes. The reporter coughed again, wiped his mouth with a hasty smudge from the sleeve of his brown overcoat that was irrevocably stained by age, lack of any attempt to clean it, and similar abuse over several years.

Chapter XII

Edge of Reason

Once again, press appeared on Matt's drive. This time, however, they knew that *he* was the story, made so much sweeter and given a life all of its own by his association with one of the most talented and sexiest women on the planet. Jealousy-fuelled thoughts appeared at the time of the wedding and held that he was simply not worthy of this wonderful woman. Stories surfaced in many of the newspapers that Fabienne had 'sold' herself too cheaply to this *nobody*, the person who had seemingly appeared from nowhere and had carried off just about the greatest prize ever to grace a rock stage. Such debates, whether right or wrong, true or otherwise, were now meaningless compared to the stories that had been given traction beyond newsmen's wildest dreams. The press appeared in force and camped out once again on his drive. Large white vans, communications vehicles with satellite dishes and booms that carried sophisticated aerials and electronic gadgetry as befitted a moon landing thousands of miles away in space, but were now attuned to a story much nearer home. Events that held the nation transfixed: this very spot was where their focus was held, round the clock, and therefore, where newsmen were directed to remain. Matt did his best to hide within the confines of the house, but even a fleeting appearance at one of the many windows brought whoops of delight from the assembled press and cameras were immediately swung in the direction indicated by excited men and women pointing to be followed by strong lighting. Throughout this time his loneliness was intensified and even harder to bear because the press now knew that Fabienne was not present. Jim Duggan's pictures had somehow captured her hurried flight of a few nights before.

Just when he was about to run out of food, he struck on the idea of an Internet shopping delivery. The poor driver who turned up in the refrigerated van had difficulty navigating a path to the front door, but this was the least of his problems. The press pack, sensing that this was some sort of ruse, subjected him to intense scrutiny. Things became even more charged when Matt opened the front door at the top of the porch, with the smooth sandstone steps, as the croed threatened to surge through. It was only when the police were called that a modicum of calm was restored.

Jim Duggan appeared and strode amongst his contemporaries, as might a Messiah amongst disciples. He had been vindicated beyond his wildest imaginings and his column had been front-page news on the *Daily Scorcher* and the *Sunday Scoop* on every issue since he had broken the story. His photographs and insight had been as well-timed and precise as a laser guided missile. He had unveiled the story in excoriating detail as his investigative beam had shone into the darkest of corners in which the GP had foolishly tried to hide. Jim Duggan had found him in each of these shadows as if guided either by the hand of God or by prescient vision. Jim had been transformed from an out of work 'has-been' who was unlikely ever to find employment again to the position of Chief Reporter; the person who was now sought after by every news agency and outlet up and down the land, finally befitting his new found status as the man who could do no wrong. Their only regret was that the star herself had vanished, and although Jim had somehow captured her hasty departure, her presence would have added still more fuel to the pyre that was now burning unrelentingly through the GP's life. Jim's star, however, was firmly in the ascendant, and his pictures and his copy were subject to outlandish bids by news agencies around the world, which were determined to hitch their wagons to the story that burned ever more intensely by the day.

Lonely, desolate feelings found Matt at precisely this time. These were even more intrusive and destructive than any enquiry that the press might make: he simply could not escape from the torturing thoughts now within. He wandered around the house, which now resembled a prison. At night he did his best to draw curtains, to frustrate the hundreds of prying lenses he knew to be out there; however, most of the time, he sat in darkness with only his own destructive loops of thought for company.

One evening he turned on the television. Fabienne had been invited to appear on a chat show. His negative thoughts had somehow now detached him emotionally as well as physically from this amazing woman, who appeared fresh and relaxed on the sofa of the talk-show host. The handsome young man, who interviewed her, appeared as spellbound with her as Matt himself had been when they had first met. The chemistry between the two of them was palpable; the atmosphere sizzled and fizzed with electricity as it might just before the release of an almighty storm when rain finally came. Initially, Fabienne had appeared just a little nervous. Wearing a short, fitted shift dress, she had trouble settling, tugging at its hem as the camera swooped low in front of her. The high-definition cameras seemed to home in on the long,

122

slim legs and the tall, sleek and pointy platform stilettos in a 'nude' colour shiny-patent leather. Then, however, as she immersed herself in the conversation she relaxed, leant back just a little, her presence shining across the entire TV studio and into the millions of homes who had tuned in to watch her being interviewed. By prior agreement, no mention was made of Matt, which only confirmed what he realised: he was now reduced to pariah status, who could only hold back the star that he had given up everything in order to help. He understood in that moment, even if, by some miracle, he was proven innocent, his presence would still damage her by association.

He stared, now transfixed, at the television. The HD image showing in the most brutal of detail: her beauty, her magnetism and the all-important, ill-defined but most vital of attributes—what some would call *star* status. Her interviewer continued to hang, spellbound on each, and every word that came forth from those pretty, lush lips that continued to sparkle almost as much as those bright eyes, which seemed to contain the secret of life itself. As Matt sat engrossed, his low mood and anxiety generated cruel thoughts that sought him out like an oil-slick appearing on a sandy beach. Just how could such a girl have settled for someone like him? Surely, such a person should be with someone as fabulous as she. No doubt, she had been hasty and was even now regretting her suggestion of marriage. Perhaps she regarded, as most stars did in today's temporary world, that the liaison was only to be for the shortest of intervals. Any fool could see it was a simple arrangement that she had struck with herself, simply in order to pay him back in some way for the assistance he had given. As a whirlwind of destructive and damaging thoughts found him and held him dead centre, the cruellest thought of all then arose. She'd never told him that she loved him. Not once. He stared again;

even blinking was suspended as this final truth ensnared him like a weary traveller being caught by a hungry Polar bear that had been stalking him across the Canadian ice floes for days. A moment of simple clarity coming to him before a swift death intervened: the weeks they'd spent in each other's company, the thousands of ideas they'd discussed and the millions of words they'd imparted, none of them, not one, had ever contained that simple four-letter word—from her. How could he have not noticed this before? It seemed this most vital sentiment had been totally lacking. Perhaps he'd been so spellbound by her company that he'd ignored what he could see now was surely a terminal rift in their relationship.

Steve had tried to warn him, had pleaded with him, that his pursuit of the sexiest and brightest star that the world had ever seen was bound to lead to self-immolation on the pyre that had once been his life. He could see it all now. Realising how stupid he must seem to others: how some would laugh, some would pity, and some would simply wonder just how long it would take him to see what the man on the Clapham omnibus had seen all along. Events then surged together: his worry, stress, the feeling of being hunted, his loneliness; the cold dark night, and now, finally, his stupidity. She'd never loved him. Just how could he have assumed that she did? This was the cruellest word of all: assumptions could make a fool of anyone—especially someone who'd been deaf as well as blind.

He stabbed at the remote to extinguish the bright scene; his mood now more at one with the darkness that immediately filled the room. He sat there for some time, his life surely over; having lost everything that was of value. Most of all, he had staked everything on the girl that he now knew no one could ever contain, and surely, like a majestic swan in a cage, no-one should

124

every try. She belonged out there, talking to handsome interviewers, standing on illuminated stages at the centre of vast arenas. Without doubt, she deserved to be seen on exotic locations with beautiful and unsullied people.

Lonely and desperate hours seemed to pass slower as if time itself had been damaged by the unremitting sadness that now occupied all his thoughts. All attempts to distract himself came to nothing. The press continued to occupy his drive just as they had done on the occasion when Rita had tipped them off to Fabienne's whereabouts. Matt's efforts to distract them at that time were not only a cruel reminder of happier times, but also emphasised that they would not be hoodwinked again.

Eventually, when he could fall no further, he remembered the act fed purely by instinct where he'd checked her fall the night she first appeared. He turned his television up to an unusually loud volume so that any reporters who remained in front of his house would be able to hear it. He went into the kitchen, having turned off the light, stole through the back entrance and through the little gate at the end of his property, seeking out the little wooden bridge with its smooth handrails. He looked up, just as he asked Fabienne to do that first night. His wretched and desolate mood insisted that he would see no more than a few stars, the light of which was now only reaching Earth long after they had burned through to the blackness of space. He knew that all he would be able to witness was in fact the end of stars and the end of him. Mercifully, the winter's night was cold and frosty but absolutely clear. His eyes opened as he accommodated the darkness. He took in the magnificence of the stars, with a single and silent gasp. Their detached nature, but calm permanence now reassuring him: they were not subject to the foolishness of men, nor in any way affected by their dark deeds.

He stood there for some time: neither feeling the cold, nor aware of the passage of time. In what must have been some time after midnight, Matt returned to his cold and lonely house, the television still shouting out to its deserted walls.

The following day after securing the first night's sleep in what seemed like weeks, he awoke feeling more refreshed. Although Matt's solicitor had instructed him to say nothing, he eventually found himself offering the reporters tea and biscuits in an attempt to keep himself busy.

That night, as he sat once again in a darkened room, he brightened visibly when he heard the latch on the gate at the back of his house. He rushed into the kitchen, turning the lights out. Through the large windows he could just about see a woman approaching the house, her implausibly black hair already blending with the gathering night. He opened the back door and couldn't resist hugging the woman as one might a firmly rooted tree in a tropical storm.

'Whoa, boy, it's only been a couple of days! Let's hope they don't send you to prison!'

'Don't joke about such things. This lot out there have me convicted already. I think any day they are going to start to erect a gallows or a guillotine or some such like.'

Fabienne returned his kiss, and for that moment his torment was suspended, albeit for the briefest interval of time, for more disquieting thoughts still refused to depart. 'Not if I've got anything to do with it, Matt, my darling.'

She took off the black wig, scratching her head as the tousled blonde locks once again re-established themselves. 'Wow, that wig is so warm. I don't think I could have worn it for much longer.'

126

'Shame, I was beginning to fancy you in that with that little black suit.'

'Get down, Matt. I think when I do my touring I'd better not leave you at home. I don't think you could last for more than a few days.' Sensing his discomfort, she changed the subject quickly. 'These coloured contact lenses are killing me. I'll just go and change and get these out of my eyes.'

A few minutes later, she joined him in the lounge. He had drawn the heavy curtains before switching on the lights so as not to attract further attention from any press who were still waiting for any further revelations from the disgraced GP. She sat next to him on the sofa. He pressed a cup of coffee and a plate complete with a slice of lemon meringue pie into her hands.

'Oh thank you, Matt, I'm famished.'

'Would you like something more substantial? Proper food?'

'No, this'll be fine. Well, just as I suspected,' she offered with a hint of triumph now residing in the bright eyes, 'your old flame, Doctor Letworth, is up to her scrawny neck in all this—and my old friend Jim Duggan.'

'So your instinct about all this was correct all along. I should have known that it's too much of a coincidence that he has managed to capture so many photographs as soon as the story broke. Talk about making the news. It brings things into a very different perspective.' He looked at his wife with unabridged admiration. The only one who'd guessed. 'How did you know it was her?'

'Intuition, Matt. I remember the day she practically pinned me to the floor to get more information from me when she thought I was your drug rep girlfriend.'

'But how can you be certain?'

'Well then, that's easy, Matt,' she nodded enthusiastically between mouthfuls of pie, using the fork as a magician might wield a wand. 'She kept looking at me, but my wonderful exaggerated French accent had her fooled. Just how many know where the cocaine was found? She offered the bottom-right drawer, and I thought to myself, *"I didn't even know that, and I'm sleeping with the guy who is supposed to have put it there!"*.'

'And Jim?'

'Trotting into her surgery like a little lap dog—a rather smelly lap dog, I might add.'

'Well, your strategy of approaching the surgery under-cover really paid off. Borrowing Jane's car was a touch of brilliance.'

'That reminds me, Matt, she is such a nice girl. I do hope she finds someone special. She seems to be so struck on you.'

He smiled, no more words came forth, but detecting a pause opening for a little too long, he continued. 'And the stocking?'

'Matt, her first mistake, I believe. I never forget smells, and that stocking had the smell of her noxious perfume all over it. If you ever do leave, don't leave me for a woman who smells like that, will you? I just couldn't bear it.'

Suddenly his smile was deflated: at once he'd been reminded of something that had been troubling him.

She detected the nuance of unabridged sadness cross his expression, and knew immediately that her return had been but a temporary distraction in something much more painful. She knew him well enough by now to approach such matters indirectly. 'So, Matt, how are you holding up?' The chestnut brown eyes, courtesy of the contact lenses, had been restored to the permanent blue of a sandy bay with deep crystal waters.

'I'm okay, Sylvie.'

She knew him too well not to detect expedient words, used to cover deeper, less comfortable feelings. '*Okay* doesn't sound like *okay* to me. In fact, it sounds much less than okay. What is it, Matt?'

'Oh, you know, being cooped up in here, the press circling, not being able to work, worries about what people think of me.'

'People, in this village, those who know you, your thousands of patients, without exception, love you. I can't go anywhere without being mobbed by your fans, and *I'm* supposed to be the star!'

He laughed but uneasy thoughts returned. 'Yes but look at the comment in the media.'

'You *are* joking? Don't you remember what a certain person once told me when he rescued me from the need for the press to pursue the story? That person who saved me when I felt as bad, almost, as he does now?' She knew that they had still not plumbed the depths that they needed to gauge. She continued. 'Besides, Matt, that isn't it. What is it, my darling? Tell me?'

Speech had become just one of the means of communication that existed between them.

'Sylvie, do you love me?'

She blinked as those mesmerising blue eyes were refreshed by a single sweep from the eyelids, and the long lashes. This was the only pause she needed to formulate a reply—or so she thought. 'Well, I'm just not sure. You know we pop stars: here today and gone tomorrow.'

His mouth fell open as he failed to anticipate her reply or the joke she'd intended.

She grabbed both his hands, the soft palms interlocking with her own, sensing that the joke had badly misfired—and this could only mean that his mood was even lower than she'd realised.

She thought that they'd had the discussion. She thought that he knew how she felt and also some of the things that she could neither say, nor admit to feeling. Not even to herself. Furthermore, she couldn't help but feel that Matt had missed the point. She'd often heard the saying that 'love was never enough'. Surely this was perfectly true: this overused word was usually voiced by teenagers, on their first date, or by women writing in glossy magazines about finding their 'soul-mate'. Fabienne very much doubted this: wondering if the words were worth as much as the paper they were printed on, and would last just about as long. And this was, of course, only until next week's issue. More than this, she believed its attractions to be overstated and illusory. Surely one should live for the here-and-now since such an emotion was a devalued currency that ultimately would buy little in today's 'price for everything' world. Without doubt, much more concrete things, such as affection, closeness, togetherness, shared experiences, and yes, sex, were enough. What more could anyone want or need? In not accepting this, she believed, people were only fooling themselves and others.

Love could end in a heartbeat, and something that was a lot less pleasant could easily replace it. Why not, therefore, concentrate on the things that were more concrete and easier to define? By lowering expectations in this way, one could surely avoid getting hurt and hurting others. She'd intended no such deception, and could only regret it now if she'd misled him. Surely as a man—and *especially* as a man—he couldn't fail to see the point. She understood in that moment that, when he was stronger, when he'd got through this—*if* he got through this—then she'd have to tell him just how she felt. And this was, she was certain, just how everyone felt. She took the view that, sooner or later, everyone would accept her view: they just weren't aware of it as yet.

If her mind was racing at this point, with a million thoughts of her own and the one that was uppermost, she tried to shield it from him. The words she wanted to say were the ones she could not speak; the ones she dare not even admit, in the loneliest of nights, to herself. Just how could he not know that she loved him more than the sun that warmed the Earth; the waves that caressed the beaches; the wind that blew air to refresh the fields, the plains and the cities. And of course the stars; the constant stars that would exist almost as long as her love for him.

She moved quickly, kicking her shoes off and kneeling on the leather sofa, now enveloping his firm neck with both hands. 'Well then, I can see that a little proof is going to be needed here, Matt.' She kissed him ever so slowly: time itself had now disengaged from the emotions she held for him deep within. She whispered tantalisingly in his right ear, her voice dropping by a semitone. 'Matt Sinclair, you are the one who believed in me when very few did. You are the one who risked everything to help me. Without you I'd be nowhere and have nothing. My life would be in ruins if it hadn't been for you.'

She continued to hold him, kissing him and whispering endearments in his ear, and yet he realised, in that moment, that something—something vital—was missing. He wondered at that juncture if it had ever been there and he had simply been swept along by events.

He looked a little embarrassed as she nodded knowingly, having uncovered a secret that he'd sought to obscure. He never wanted to be away from her, never ever.

He kissed her but knew that a vital ingredient had escaped the two of them, and he understood that he could probably not

131

continue without it. As was his way, when faced with an impasse, he changed subject. 'So what do we know so far? What can we prove?' he asked.

'We know she's involved but we just have no proof that she is the one, and of course mister vile *scoop* man.'

'I just don't know she seems to have been pretty thorough. Just how can we prove that it's a stitch-up?'

'She'll have made a mistake somewhere, you see. She's not that good,' Fabienne assured him.

Matt nodded as positively as he could, yet something told him deep within that uncovering proof might well be elusive and unfortunately, moves to suspend him permanently, to prosecute him and of course to strike him off the medical register were already gathering pace. They desperately needed a breakthrough—and soon.

'Well, Sylvie, your instinct about Rita was excellent and, of course, so was your disguise.'

'You leave my little black suit alone!' she smiled. 'You are in quite enough trouble as it is. Maybe I'll put it on when it's your birthday or maybe sooner, if you are good.'

'I'm always good,' he offered as he kissed her once again.

'Let's sleep on it and see how we feel in the morning, and if you are really good in the depths of the night I'll whisper sweet nothings until you fall asleep.'

In his low moments, Matt had forgotten what he had learned, as if by instinct, about this woman that filled his life, his thoughts, his hopes and his dreams. She had revealed to him on many occasions the frightened young girl who had seen jealousy and suspicion destroy what she had believed was undefiled love; how quickly she had learned otherwise, and with knowledge had come fear—fear that had stalked every relationship that she had ever

132

embarked upon, until one day she had met a man who had risked all for her. Perhaps this was all there was, and he was foolish to expect anything more. He hadn't grasped that she would happily settle for the features of a relationship that would not let her down. At its most simple, love was a luxury that she could not afford. For him, on the other hand, it was the very essence of a relationship: without it, there was no relationship.

He knew again by instinct that she wasn't ready to discuss such matters, and that other events were now impacting with much more moment on their lives. The day would come, and soon, when they could not avoid the discussion that held the key to their future lives. Clarifying this would either cement their relationship or would lead to its dissolution. He concluded that this must be how many mega stars ran their lives: with purely superficial thoughts and emotions. He realised, in that moment, that this was why so many failed—and so quickly. He could not understand just how he had been so stupid. The only answer to his question was one that would continue to elude him: his thoughts were based on wholly incorrect assumptions—ones which, if not corrected, would do more harm than the person intent on discrediting him.

Matt and Fabienne had promised that they would address the problem of Rita, and of Jim Duggan's resurgence, the following morning, but more brutal events were set to intrude.

Chapter XIII

Arrest

The police came early, almost like a dawn raid on a drug den in inner-city Salford. The delight of the assembled reporters and pressmen knew no bounds. Instinct had told them that it would be expeditious to hang on, to maintain their thirsty vigil for more news. Jim Duggan had appeared in person just moments before. It was now clear that a man of his exalted status had been given access to inside information that they would have to continue to search for.

Police cars appeared in force as they swept into the drive, the gravel protesting as if it had been whipped up by a whirlwind. Even more delight came the photographers' way when Fabienne appeared at the door in the thinnest of chemises, and in an unguarded moment, the wind and harsh winter light had allowed the capture of photographs that added more sauce to the story. Moments later, Matt was led away on his way to Denton Police Station where he was to be charged with conspiring to commit fraud. The MHRA had reviewed the material submitted by Eltraset Pharm, and had decided that the full weight of the law should be applied in this case. A case of brazen fraud that the agency, in conjunction with the pharmaceutical company, was intending to pursue vigorously, where failure to do so would damage the whole multi-billion pharmaceutical industry of the United Kingdom. They knew that one rogue GP could never be allowed to endanger that and the only course of action now was a very public and vigorous pursuit through the judicial process.

Jim Duggan smiled like a gargoyle, his grisly expression breaking through the tired and cracked facial skin. He knew the tide had turned for him. These two had outwitted him for the last time, and they were both about to pay the price in full. Pictures of her looking ravishing, distressed, but in a relative state of undress would sell to the foreign tabloids for a small fortune, and Jim's name would be on all of them. Their importance, however, would pale beside the priceless value of the ones he had taken of the rogue, thieving GP. He spat out a considerable quantity of spittle as he licked his lips and prepared them to receive a celebratory cigarette, which he lit with unabated delight. His peers too had now started to look to him as their better, a leader amongst frail men. Eyes were averted as he passed his colleagues; tones were hushed in his presence with almost a reverence. People were respectful, waited for him to speak and, above all, made space for him, like a professional golfer being afforded the honour of the first stroke.

Another person was also ecstatically happy as she caught the lunchtime news: there were pictures of Matt being driven to the police station and his solicitors hurrying inside as they struggled to keep pace with the rip-tide that had now all but drowned him. Rita knew that the end game was now in sight. There was no way he could recover from this, and all that would be left would be a little flotsam: the sole remnants of his once cocky and vaunted life. A life that was practically all but over. The sweetest part of her revenge on him was the fact that she had detected that it would also destroy the puerile bimbo, and neither her mediocre singing voice, nor her scantily clad form plastered across glossy magazines would save her.

She wondered if Matt now regretted spurning her very attractive offers of work. He could have been at the pinnacle of a long and illustrious career, if he had taken her offer and her advice. He deserved the fate that was now closing on him with the eagerness of a pack of wolves detecting the scent of a stumbling traveller in deep snow. How could he have turned down her offer—turned *her* down? She hoped he would regret this single act of folly for the rest of his miserable and now worthless life.

Rita's instinct had been as equally powerful as her prescience. Matt's name duly appeared in all the newspapers the following day and not for the first time. The *Daily Scorcher* and that Sunday the *Sunday Scoop* seemed to be in the vanguard of such stories. Their owner, Mervyn Boomer, was invited on to *Newsnight* for his views on the temporary and fragile nature of stardom and the inappropriate liaisons that such stars seemed to attract. His interview was measured, insightful and impactful and it was only off-camera that he permitted himself the smile of satisfaction and of cold, calculating undiluted revenge.

Once again, but this time, purely by association, Fabienne was damaged. Rather than the victim of a simple mistake, she was portrayed as one lacking in even the fundamentals of decision-making. In portraying her as a vacuous air-head the newsmen, led by the *Daily Scorcher* successfully moved the focus from her talent, her loyal fan base, the business acumen she had brought to her financial affairs and of course the occult but charitable acts that she had personally set in place. The extensive list of her kind and wonderful attributes were then deconstructed by lacerating column inches, in newspapers that sold in their thousands—and all at her expense.

Matt was charged but allowed home on bail provided he made no attempt to visit the surgery. The police passed a file to the General Medical Council. Though not a case of medical negligence, the GMC charged each doctor with the responsibility for conducting themselves in a manner as befitted their professional status and also one that reflected at all times the trust that the public had a right to place on their shoulders. A hastily convened session at the GMC had found unanimously that Dr Sinclair was most likely in breach of this trust. Papers were served pending a full hearing. Matt was given notice that such a panel had the authority to strike him from the medical register, and he was warned to expect such an event. Moreover as this was a case of fraud, his defence union were not retained to represent him and though he was allowed counsel, any pleas for leniency were most likely to fall on deaf ears. Quite apart from the loss of his reputation, disgrace was only one of the things likely to be heaped upon him. Legal counsel warned Matt, that if a prosecution was secured, as seemed likely; then fines and legal costs were likely to be substantial. Fabienne, too, was approached hurriedly by her many financial advisers. Any fines imposed on her husband would also fall to her, and it was not inconceivable that both of them could be ruined. She was advised to create a firewall between her finances and those of her husband. She looked engagingly at the men in suits who surrounded the table in the meeting room, as they presented their case and their recommendations. Still smiling, she thanked them for their time and for their advice, but whilst seeing the financial advantages of such a move, would be unlikely to follow it. She remembered the time when her management company was in free-fall on the Stock Market and Matt had invested his entire funds in a move simply to show solidarity with someone he hardly knew. She reasoned that it was now time to repay the favour. She informed her advisers that not only would she not be creating a firewall, but that her entire resources would be devoted to proving his innocence. They looked at each other nervously. Gazing back at her deliberatively, they couldn't help but wonder if she had just made a rational decision or if perhaps her mental state had been affected by the proceedings.

Matt and Fabienne sensed that they were at an impasse; the answer to the puzzle that lay before them as elusive as ever. They were also acutely aware that if they did not solve it, and soon, then being struck off the medical register would be the least of the punishments that awaited the GP. As always, at such time, it made sense to journey to Steve and Mary's house to see if any progress could be made.

'I know that you know it's Rita, Sylvie, but we need proof!' The frustration was evident in Steve's voice.

'She's bound to have slipped up. There must be something we can do,' came from Fabienne.

'I agree there must be a way to rescue poor Matt,' declared Steve.

It was these words that stung Matt the most; he had now been reduced to an object of pity. He knew that it was quite unintentional on the part of his friend, but he remained quiet, almost as if resigned to his fate.

'Jim Duggan, surely *he*'s the weak spot,' offered Mary.

'I agree,' said Steve, 'but proof, my love, proof.'

A pleasant evening, not for the first time, was hijacked by worries. Worries that seemed insoluble and the whiff of a career in terminal decline lay heavily in the atmosphere.

Mary in particular refused to allow the evening to proceed without the slightest glimmer of hope. She could see the couple look more and more dejected as the evening passed. She waited for her opportunity, just as the pair got up to leave. She moved quickly to Fabienne, despite her unaccustomed bulk and weight, and grabbed her arm, nestling it against her tummy. 'Now don't forget, Miss Fabienne, our plans for this week. We said we were going to continue with our cookery skills?' she beamed at the pop star expectantly.

Fabienne wanted to cry off in order to spend more time with Matt, but the look from Mary assured her that this would be unwise. After the slightest pause, as she recognised that look from Mary, she nodded, smiled and said, 'Yes, yes of course. I am so looking forward to it.'

Mary was far too good a judge of the human condition for her not to notice the effort and pain that Fabienne had expunged in order to construct that simple sentence, but she responded with a warm hug and kissed Fabienne just as they departed. Ultimately, Mary understood one thing that was as vital as each breath she took. She accepted the young woman's desire to stand by her husband come what may, but she also sensed her need to put her own troubled past behind her. Rita had instinctively understood that by damaging Matt, she would also disable, perhaps fatally, his wife too. Mary patted her stomach; she felt a particularly active sequence of kicks, and also significant tightening from her abdomen. She knew that they would have find some answers fairly soon if the two of them were not to be obliterated. Just as the magnificent car started and the reversing lights blinked on, she understood one very important fact of the game then in play. If it was to come down to a simple choice, his life for hers, then Fabienne would make that exchange: just as he would for her.

Arrest

A few days later, Steve was finishing his clinic when an urgent call was received. His secretary buzzed through to him even though usual protocol was not to interrupt the psychologist's consultations.

'It's a Doctor Letworth, Doctor Collins. I am so sorry to disturb you in this way.'

'Could I phone her back, Sally?'

'No, she says it's urgent and it won't wait. I'm sorry about this, Doctor Collins. She insisted that I put her through without delay. She was rather rude, I must say.'

'Oh, very well then.' Steve apologised to his patient and stepped out of the room and into the office in order to take the call. This was a great shame as the patient was finally ready after weeks and many consultations to start opening up to him, Steve at last gaining the impression that some progress was about to be made.

'Rita, what can I do for you?'

'About time too. I have been waiting for ages for you to come to this phone. Don't you know I am a busy person and I haven't got the time to be sitting round all day waiting for you hospital doctors to amble along to the phone.'

'Yes, Rita, I do apologise, but I was with a patient, and my secretary's instructions are not to interrupt me unless there is an emergency.'

'A likely story. Do you think I'm stupid? Do you say that to your stupid friend? Bet he swallows that line, hook and sinker.'

'Well, Rita, it happens to be the truth. Now where were we? Are you alright, Rita?'

'Yes, of course, you buffoon—unlike that stupid friend of yours.'

Steve Collins was known to have a very sensitive and specific antenna when he was dealing with patients who were on the verge of acute psychiatric illness. Such sensitivity was barely needed now: he detected a worrying and deteriorating mood from the female GP. He knew that he needed more information and carefully opened his line of questions to draw her out more.

'Who is that, Rita?'

'Don't be so stupid. You know exactly who I am talking about so don't play coy with me. Now are you going to see this patient or not?'

'Yes, of course, Rita. Would you be so kind as to give me the details?'

'Don't try to be all smarmy with me.'

'I was wondering if you were okay, Rita. You seem very upset. Is there something you'd like to discuss with me?'

'Don't you dare try your psycho-babble with me. I eat stupid prats like you for breakfast. You bloody psychologists spend all day talking whilst we GPs get on with real work.'

Steve's active mind was now churning with so many thoughts. 'Are you sure you're okay, Rita?'

'If you ask me that once more I'm going to put in an official complaint with your hospital managers.'

'Very well then, Rita. Please give me the details.'

'Well this fifty-six year old bloody idiot says he cannot leave the house without organising everything in fours.'

'How do you mean, Rita?'

'Don't be so bloody stupid. You are as stupid as that ex-doctor friend of yours. He is stupid just like you.'

'Go on, Rita, how do you mean? Do you want to talk about your patient or something else?'

'Well, this bloody idiot has to organise everything on the shelf in the kitchen and on the hall-table into fours before he can leave for work. It's taking the silly bugger an hour to get out of the house.'

'Seems like a simple Obsessive Compulsive Disorder, Rita.'

'I know that, you effin idiot, and he needs a shrink, like you, to sort out his effin mind.'

'Very well then, Rita, I'll see him in my next clinic.'

'About bloody time too.'

'Okay, Rita, thank you for your call.'

'Don't soft-soap me, you buffoon, or you'll end up on the scrap heap like Sinclair, too.'

'How is that, Rita?'

'Don't try to trick me you bastard.' The phone clicked dead, their conversation was over.

Steve finished the interrupted consultation with his patient and immediately telephoned Parkvale Medical Centre. He was put though to Carol Thornley, one of Rita's partners.

'Hi, Steve, what can I do for you?'

Steve explained the difficult telephone conversation he'd had with Dr Letworth, and asked if anyone had noticed strange behaviour from her.

'No, nothing obvious at work. She is working all hours God sends, and she is a bit more abrasive than usual—even for her. All the staff and the patients are a bit scared of her but that's nothing new.'

'Sorry to trouble you, Carol, but I was wondering if she was on the edge of a psychotic breakdown?'

'No, can't say that I have noticed anything like that but of course I'll keep my eyes and ears open.'

Carol knew that Steve was a good friend to Matt Sinclair. She thought that he must be under enormous pressure. Surely, there were two sides to every story. Besides, it was neither her place nor her job to report erratic behaviour from one of her colleagues. She knew that, for anyone who went up against Dr Letworth, it would go badly, and she wasn't going to be the one who blew the whistle. Yes, lots of patients had practically run from her consultation room. Many, even the men, were in tears, so shocked, they were pale when they presented back at reception. Some had been asked if they wanted to rebook or to make a complaint, but then real fear had appeared in their eyes at the very mention of Dr Letworth, and most had wandered off in a sense of numbed confusion. Some had left the list and not been seen at Parkvale ever again. All this information she decided to keep to herself. She didn't want to get involved, and if Steve was trying to implicate Dr Letworth in some way, she definitely didn't want to get involved.

'Sorry, I cannot be of more help to you, Steve.'

'Oh, that's okay, Carol, just a thought. Thank you for taking my call.'

Steve was one of the most brilliant clinical psychologists of his generation. His acute mind was capable of separating the one tiny piece of information, whether that was derived from face-to-face consultation or via the telephone. He detected unabridged fear on the part of Rita's partner, but how to take things forward? He knew almost immediately that Carol was lying. Her words and reassurance were pushed just a little too hard as if she were trying to sell him a believable version of events rather than the ones she knew to be true. The more he thought about his call from Rita, the more worried he became—but how to take action? If one of Rita's partners had voiced no suspicions, then it would be very difficult for him to move things forward? Any attempts at scrutinising Dr Letworth would be seen as vindictive and motivated by concern for his friend. One thing he recognised with certainty was that Dr Letworth was on the edge of a serious mental breakdown.

Chapter XIV

Locked-In Secret

The following Monday, a bright-red open-top Alfa Giulietta Spider appeared in the car park. Though originally manufactured in 1957, it had been beautifully and painstakingly rebuilt. No expense had been spared in doing so, with original, restored parts used throughout. The couple in the car had elected to leave the roof down: though the day was a frosty December day, the bright sunshine had refused to be vanquished by the appearance of winter. The heater had done its best to warm the two occupants; however, neither had felt the least bit cold as they had made their way to the newly refurbished and extended surgery. The young woman vacated the right-hand passenger side of the vehicle. Standing there just for a moment whilst she composed herself, she gently folded her silk scarf into her handbag and waved excitedly to the driver. The car sped off with a sharp toot from the horn, and she hurried inside the surgery.

Mrs Simpson almost didn't recognise the woman with the vivid red hair that had been allowed to grow out to its lustrous and thick potential. Sunshine had partially bleached those wondrous locks, thereby creating natural highlights. Bright green eyes shone as she approached reception. Though her pale complexion was at all times resistant to even limited sun exposure, her face was sun-kissed, creating a radiance and a healthy glow that was apparent even before the uplifting smile that readily visited her face.

'Janice!'

Mrs Simpson shot round the counter and in to the waiting room. Before more words could form, she hugged the young receptionist. 'You look wonderful, Janice!' She extended her right arm and positioned the woman at the furthest edge of its travel so she could look approvingly at the wonderful shift dress and the Italian sandals on her feet. 'Janice, I am speechless. You look delightful and so grown up!' Instinct was applied but was hardly needed: for the more senior woman instantly detected that the girl had taken on the attributes of a sassy and vital young woman.

'I take it you have had a nice holiday. How are your parents?'

'They are well, thank you, Mrs Simpson. My dad sends his best wishes to you. I wanted to thank you. Thank you from the bottom of my heart, for letting me go. I don't know what would have happened if I hadn't gone in that moment.'

'No, not at all, Janice. Besides, I couldn't bear to see you so upset, those pretty eyes overflowing with such torment.'

Janice smiled but did not respond to the mounting look of curiosity on her boss's face.

Mrs Simpson reflected on the acute distress in which she had found the younger woman not more than four weeks ago. In a rare moment of absolute clarity, a simple, single conclusion formed in the manager's mind. 'I detect that's all in the past.'

'Yes, I can assure you of that. It was so kind of you to let me go, with no notice, and with things here in such a critical state. Forgive me, I hope I didn't drop everyone in it, did I?'

Mrs Simpson beamed at her young colleague, her curiosity now overflowing: she wanted to talk of other things. 'Of course not.'

'So, how are things here?'

'Terrible, Janice, worst possible.'

'Oh my goodness, I'm so sorry. Is it because I left you in the lurch?' Her hands came up to frame her mouth as guilt and regret appeared in force on her expression.

'You haven't heard then?' Mrs Simpson couldn't quite defeat the smile, as she loved nothing more than to pass on gossip and scandal on to the unaware.

'No, we got back off the ferry late last night. We drove all night. Heard what?'

'Sit down, Janice, I have terrible news. Doctor Sinclair has been charged with fraud. They say he's cheated on the study people—he's defrauded them—and all for a few thousand pounds. Can you believe such a thing?'

'No, I can't! I can't believe he'd *ever* do anything like that!' Janice offered with neither a hint of delay nor doubt.

'But *how* do you know?' her boss asked, incredulously, as if she needed to understand the nature of such blind faith.

'I know him, Mrs S, and so do you. I'd trust him with every penny I had. I'd trust him with my life,' she said, detecting that her boss was perhaps revelling in all this just a little too much.

'But, Janice these are strange times, you know. Since he married the megastar perhaps he's changed?'

'No, sorry Missus S, I can't see that. Some people won't change, and he's one of those people. I know that—and so do you.' Faith, one of the most elusive facets of human nature and yet one of the most powerful, especially when absolute, as now, shone from Janice. The simple words awakened her boss from the trance that she'd been unwittingly trapped in.

'Yes of course, you are right,' she accepted, seemingly a little stunned at first, and then nodded, finally ready to agree with her young colleague.

'So how has this come about?'

'Well, it all began when they collected the study folders. The drug reps are not allowed to remove them unless they are sealed. There are little tamper-proof tags on each of the bags, where the zip ends. When these are snapped off you can then tell if they have been opened in transit, I suppose before they are opened at Eltraset Pharm headquarters. Anyway, I'm told that when they broke the seals to open one of Doctor Sinclair's bags, they discovered that he'd falsified lots of records.'

Janice's shock prevented her from detecting that the manager still hadn't quite grasped the situation. 'Are you serious, Mrs S? I just can't see him doing anything like that even before he met *you know who*,' she said in a slightly hushed voice, as if it were still a secret, 'and certainly not now when he's got so much in his life. Do you think he's been framed in some way or could they have made a mistake?'

'Well, I can't see that, Janice.'

'Surely it's the *only* thing that makes sense? He isn't capable of doing those things. We all know that,' she reminded her boss with wisdom belying her young years. 'I remember the last thing I asked him was whether I could do a surgery website. He insisted on paying me, even though it was a project for my college course. He then went on to the computer to order a new camera so I could take some quality images of the new surgery. He ordered it there and then, got out his own plastic. That isn't a man who is about to defraud the study company. I'd bet my life on him,' Janice said,

148

nodding as if she still needed to persuade her boss of the man's innocence.

'How much is involved?'

'Nine-hundred a form and they say there may be twenty forms.'

'Surely, that's peanuts to him—and certainly to Miss Fabienne!'

'Well, Janice, they have arrested, charged and have suspended him. We have new doctors working here now, and poor Doctor Stevens doesn't know where he is!'

'Oh I think he'll cope, *somehow*, Mrs S,' she offered with more of an edge to her voice than she intended.

'The poor patients, too, are in shock. They have a signed petition out in reception and also in the village. They are all saying he's innocent, like you, but it'll do no good. It's gone too far for that now. They say he's going to be prosecuted and then they'll strike him off. Most likely he'll do time and he'll never work again. They say it's all her fault, every man she touches, it all goes belly-up.'

Janice shook her head; she didn't want to hear any more. Mrs Simpson had simply offered what had happened as irrefutable proof that their boss must be guilty. Janice knew that he was the last person on earth who'd do such a thing. It made no sense at all, and if some people could not see that then more fool them. The other point that she couldn't agree with was the fact that Miss Fabienne was in any way to blame for these events. She'd seen the two of them together, and she recognised it for what it was— something very, very special.

Janice sat down heavily at her workstation in the newly-fitted office. She opened her desk drawer, and pulled out the new digital camera she'd placed in there just a few short weeks before. She brushed its aluminium case between her finger and thumb, caressing the smooth, quality finish that denoted a substantial piece of kit. This was the last thing her boss had given her, and only a short interval before she'd fled from the surgery. She remembered how kind he'd been to her; this was not the hallmark of someone who was then about to commit fraud. She sighed a long sigh, temporarily granted prescient vision because she saw the new surgery, now, as a wasteland. 'Well, we won't be needing these images. I'd taken some images of the staff and lots around the surgery. I was planning to use them for the new website. It seems like a non-starter now that poor Doctor S has been banjaxed in this way.' She flicked the camera on and started clicking through the images, preparing to delete them. 'Wow, lots of images here—and all of them taken in happier times. Hang on, who's that?' she pointed at the screen, one of the images she neither remembered nor recognised.

Mrs Simpson peered myopically at the small screen. 'No use asking me, Janice, must be a patient. Just delete them.'

Her finger remained, poised over the delete button. 'Not a patient I recognise in that filthy mac. He doesn't look like a workman. What do you think?'

'Nothing, Janice, I don't think anything. Just delete them and let's get on with some work. We'll have surgeries starting soon.'

'Look, Mrs S!' Janice stood, placing the camera literally under her boss's nose in her eagerness.

Somewhat impatiently and reluctantly, the manager at last reached for her glasses that, she'd discovered, had been on a long chain round her neck at the outset. She gazed at the little screen that Janice held up for her inspection, now in focus, courtesy of her reading glasses. Small, grey eyes widened to the point of incredulity. She pointed at the screen excitedly, suddenly feeling
150

breathless. 'Janice, I think I have something here! Do you know who that is?'

'No,' said Janice a little suspiciously, sensing that, suddenly, the provenance of the image was about to be switched.

'That, my young friend,' she said triumphantly as she crossed he arms across her ample bosom, leaning back a little to counterbalance the weight, 'is Jim Duggan!'

'Jim Duggan, the newsman? What's he doing here?'

If Mrs Simpson had lagged behind the curve of discovery, and if she'd been a little slow to discover just who had been in their midst that long autumn, she redressed the imbalance with aplomb. Her voice went up a semitone; her eyes sparkled with new-found learning if not intelligence. Her head nodded back and forth at its most irritating: affirmation that here were the facts everyone had been searching for.

'He,' she hesitated just as long as she was able, until the suspense nearly killed her, let alone the agony of expectation in which she'd plunged her young colleague, 'is the man who has been crowing from every front page. He is the one who has appeared in just the right place, and just at the right time, every time—or so it would appear. This, my young friend, is the man who brought poor Doctor Sinclair down singlehandedly. His photos, so they tell me, have been bought up by news agencies around the globe—and he's been in *our* surgery unannounced and uninvited. Upon my word!' Her hand now came forward whilst pointing to the camera: as an assassin might point to the high-velocity rifle from which he'd just fired the round that had despatched some unmentionable despot.

'Oh my!' was all Janice could manage as the enormity of what she'd just heard couldn't be fully compassed by her overawed mind.

In days gone by Mrs Simpson would have swept forward as she granted her audience more and more sensational exposition of precisely what was in progress, right under their noses. The manager, however, still hadn't quite grasped the full extent of the changes that a few short weeks had brought about in her young colleague. Sharp young eyes pointed to the pixelated image on the little screen on the back of the camera. Their green glow was now resonating with their owner, like an elixir of life.

'What's that he's carrying?' Green eyes shone with the precision of an argon laser as the young receptionist detected the most vital piece of evidence. 'It looks like a—'

'Print it! Janice, print it,' were the final words Mrs Simpson could manage before Janice seized control of the discovery that would soon cause events to turn.

'I can't, Mrs S, the printers here won't do it!'

She thought frantically. Surely the problem could be overcome. 'Hold on, though.'

Opening her drawer with a sharp pull and rummaging inside for what seemed like an age, she produced a lead. One end of the lead was plugged into a little socket in the camera and the other slotted into a compatible port in one of the computers. She summoned the camera to life excitedly. Within seconds, a large image appeared filling the computer screen. Jim Duggan was revealed in all his distasteful glory. 'Look, Mrs S, he's carrying a blue study folder! *And* he's bringing it *in* to the surgery.'

'Yes, of course, Janice,' Mrs Simpson managed before the final facet of information that Janice had just revealed, which would seemingly decide the fate of man's very existence.

Janice was now calm, her voice dry, almost smoky, as once again she pointed to the enlarged image on screen.

'Look, Missus S, the security tabs—they've been pulled. He brought in *sealed* bags!' With calm had come almost perfect enlightenment because Janice now understood from being absent for four weeks all that had happened, and why, in the surgery. Most vitally, she had uncovered the final link in the puzzle that had been used to destroy her boss.

The manager shot her a glance as a defeated warrior might acknowledge the one who'd vanquished him. For once she could neither summon a knowing nod nor proprietorial words, covering the momentous discovery. As a further sign of her gathering maturity, only the slightest glance from Janice signified that she understood the moment had passed to her. Receiving it with the placidity and unassuming calm that only the experience of a river of heartbroken tears could have created.

In the final act of magnanimity, she looked at her boss. 'What should we do now?'

Mrs Simpson recovered quickly. 'Well, we need to inform Doctor Sinclair at once.'

Mrs Simpson went to the staff-room. She knew that one or two of the girls were having a last-minute coffee before starting their shifts. She informed them using few but urgently pitched words that she and Janice were going to have to vacate the premises on vital business. Both receptionists viewed the unusually animated figure of their boss with some surprise but numbness and shock brought about affirming nods, nevertheless.

Both women raced round to the GP's house, Mrs Simpson revving the little engine in her Nissan Micra with unaccustomed vigour. Within minutes, however, they were entering the large drive. A few press were still present—one or two, who had understood that they were about to issue the last rites to the GP, his career and, most likely, his freedom.

A few cameras fired off as Fabienne and Matt arrived at the door.

Matt hugged both women, as did Fabienne. Both assumed that this was purely a social call. Though amazed at the transformation in the young receptionist, they instantly detected the final secret that Janice harboured within, having recognised the same emotions within themselves. Especially long hugs were reserved for the young visitor as both recognised her deliverance from painful heart-rending trauma.

Janice held the little camera, but had something to say. First she wanted to thank her boss for showing such faith in her. Now was as good a time as any. Most of all she wanted him to know that, in a way, he'd saved himself.

'Thank you, Doctor Sinclair. You insisted on buying a new camera for my web page pictures. My old camera would never have captured such random images in such quality as this. Thank you for encouraging and supporting me in the way you did. Just as you always do with all of us.' Only then did she fire-up the camera, its bright screen flaring into life and displaying an image that represented justice, truth and freedom in one tiny rectangle.

Matt was a little unsure as to exactly what he was looking at. Weeks of being forced almost into self-imposed exile had blunted his emotions and his affect. As Janice shimmered in the room before him, he soon understood just what the young woman had discovered.

'I was just shooting random pictures, Doctor Sinclair. I wanted some unusual, unscripted images of the surgery to convey its relaxed atmosphere. I didn't even see Mister Duggan, but yet, look, here he is.'

Matt still wasn't quite sure how an image of a disgraced reporter, entering his surgery, could be important.

154

'Doctor Sinclair, have you a printer?' Janice asked, excitedly.

A few moments later, Janice succeeded in printing a 10x8 image of the secret that had lain locked in the camera, and in her office drawer, for weeks.

Matt passed the image to Fabienne. Her mouth opened as a reflection of the shock as her eyes flared even wider than usual.

Janice was a little overawed by the presence of the pop star, but Fabienne was at her best when faced with star-struck fans. She sat next to the receptionist, insisted that she call her Sylvie, as Janice had stuttered a little and most importantly the blue-crystal gaze locked on the bright-green eyes of the young woman as she blinked uncertainly in the company of someone she'd worshipped since she was a little girl.

'So what's the significance of the security tabs?' Fabienne asked, never having seen one of the blue study bags.

'Well, Fab— uh, Sylvie,' Janice began, 'the tabs are tamper-proof tabs. They are removed just prior to being removed by the drug firm in order to prevent what's happened from happening.'

'You mean fraud!'

Janice was rewarded by the wondrous smile that she had seen light up vast packed arenas on more occasions than she could remember.

'That's amazing! You're both fantastic,' Fabienne beamed.

Matt was deep in thought but sensed that his ordeal was finally over. He wasn't sure whether to laugh or cry. It was perhaps understandable that he had underestimated precisely what danger he was in. Unfortunately, he failed to foresee that he was now in much more danger than ever. Fabienne, too, could be forgiven for thinking that here was the break they needed. Matt spoke first.

'I'm sure the police would be interested in this new evidence, Janice. Thank you so much.' He hugged her once again.

Janice felt herself welling up. Dr Sinclair had always been so kind to her over the years that she'd known him. She knew him to be incapable of the things that Mrs Simpson had told her were appearing daily in the newspapers during her absence. She wanted to tell him what a superb boss and what a wonderful person he was and had been. She knew that she could never voice such things, especially in such company, but she was delighted that she'd uncovered something that would probably save him. Little could she know that this was precisely what would put him in even greater danger. Mercifully, Matt's mind was now turning with the next steps, as yet ignorant of the horror that awaited him.

Mrs Simpson stood to go, and somewhat reluctantly so did Janice.

'Janice, just before you go, come with me?' Fabienne led her from the morning room and upstairs. Fifteen minutes later, both women returned. Janice was wearing a smile of sheer delight, carrying a precious box that she held very tightly, as might a little girl on her birthday. Fabienne glowed with even more excitement: a work that was in progress had been given a great boost.

Fabienne thanked them both and escorted them to the door, whilst Matt contacted the police to pass on the newly discovered information. Fabienne returned and put her arms around him, kissing him as he finished his call.

'The police say they'll take a look, but they don't see how it proves anything.'

Fabienne looked again at the pictures. 'No, I don't think they'll be saying that when they see these. Seem pretty implicating to me.' She kissed him again.

'Wow, did you see how much Janice has changed?' he posed.

'Yes, she seems very much in love, and she really seems to have grown up of late.'

'What did you give her?'

'Did you see those shoes she was wearing? They weren't quite right and they looked so uncomfortable. I gave her a pair of mine, which are much more suitable and also gave her some pointers to walk better with a more upright posture.

'So that's what the clattering was on the landing. You women and your shoes!'

'Yes, and you men love them nearly as much.'

'Only when you are in them, my love.'

Fabienne sensed a change of subject was needed at this point and, fortuitously, remembered something she'd been bursting to ask. 'Did you say she was in love with Greg? But I thought he'd rejected her?

'Yes, indeed. She was last seen, the poor soul, leaving work in a hurry because she was so distressed. Things must have changed for her. She went to Italy with her parents.'

'That's what I could smell on her—it's Giorgio Armani. Well then, whatever. She's in love now—with someone!'

'Good job you are so good with your perfumes,' he offered, as he thought of the stocking that she had found in the back of his car.

'Yes, good job, too, I'm not the jealous type,' she said, sensing his thoughts. 'I could have gone straight to a solicitor with that one for the big *D*.'

'No one would have ever believed that I could cheat on you, or that anyone ever would want to cheat on you,' he suggested.

'Mm, good answer, Doctor Sinclair. You know just what to say.'

'It's all true, every word.'

'It'd better be. Mary's been teaching me some pretty mean tricks with a rolling pin.'

He laughed again.

Chapter XV

Absolute Discretion

Matt was quite correct: the police seemed reluctant to change their initial conclusions. As far as they were concerned, they'd charged the man they knew to be responsible. However, Matt's solicitors insisted they interview Jim Duggan. Initially Jim was tight-lipped and denied ever going near the place. When shown the pictures, he suggested that he might have dropped off supplies there one day, but nothing more. When shown a magnified print of him carrying study bags, which had been sealed, his story unravelled further. Finally his version of events seemed as hazy as his concocted story was inconsistent.

The final proof came when Matt's solicitors asked that the transport bags be examined forensically. On the outside of the incriminating bag, a small speck of dried spittle was found which was a match for Jim's DNA. When confronted with this, he then started singing like a canary and revealed that none of it was his idea. He'd been acting on the expressed wishes of Dr Letworth, who'd insisted that this was the only way to get his job back. A single strand of hair was found inside the bag, which matched her DNA.

The case against Matt collapsed just as quickly as the one against the reporter and the female GP rose. Jim was arrested by the police and charged with perverting the course of justice. Rita too was arrested, suspended from practice while the case against her was investigated.

For once the *Daily Scorcher* and the *Sunday Scoop* fell behind the curve of up-to-the-minute press releases and stories. Other newspapers, still smarting from lagging behind the publications owned by Mervyn Boomer, now forged ahead. Not only did such newspapers have a much less gossipy, sensationalist style, but they were also regarded as printing news that would bear more detailed scrutiny. Matt's innocence rode this tide beautifully.

Matt made a low-key return to the surgery a few days later. All the staff - and many patients - attended to welcome him and show support. Matt was a little nervous when Fabienne turned up with enough cake and pastries for everyone. The treats that she'd brought smelt delightful, but he'd been caught out on many previous occasions when the smell of the food was betrayed quite comprehensively by the all-important taste test. He knew that his wife had been visiting Mary with increasing frequency of late, and that Mary would have proven to be a patient teacher and Fabienne, no doubt a keen and dutiful pupil. But would it be enough? However, at that juncture, memories of dishes that he'd sat behind and realised that he simply could not eat came to visit him; once contemplated, significant stomach-churning anxiety rose inwardly. Holding his breath, while some of the guests started eating, his delight knew no bounds when he witnessed most of the plates were being cleared rather than hidden behind the nearest potted plant. He caught Fabienne detecting the mixture of shock, relief and delight as it crossed his face.

Janice was on the late shift that day. The sleek Alfa Romeo once again turned into the car park, but whilst the driver looked round for a parking spot, she hurried inside.

She wore a pale-green belted silk dress with a gold watermark overlying the fabric. The delicate gold sandals she sported clipped satisfyingly as they made contact with the surgery floor. Not only did her new sandals fit her perfectly, but also her walk was relaxed, comfortable and erect. Her whole image held something of sheer, carefree delight, as only one who was young and in love could display. Heads turned and turned again as she entered; her glorious hair aflame under the surgery down lighters and her pale-green eyes shimmering with new-found happiness.

Fabienne met her at the door and looked approvingly. She kissed her and, as she did so, whispered, 'Beautiful shoes. They really suit you.'

Janice whispered back, 'Thank you so much. They are the most amazing things I have ever owned.'

Fabienne moved back to let her enter the reception, but whilst the two women's gaze was still locked, she gently touched her own chin with an upward movement. Janice quickly understood and raised her head just a little so that the neck was straightened and the posture became much more erect.

Greg had clearly been waiting for her, because he arrived in reception as soon as she appeared. He asked her to come into his consulting room, quietly closing the new heavy fire door behind them. She sat on the patient's chair as he pointed towards it. Greg sat on the desk directly in front of her, looking very nervous and almost contrite.

'Janice, I am so sorry. I have been a complete fool. I can't believe I said those things. I must have been out of my mind. Is it too late for us?'

'Please don't say any more, Greg. You did me a favour. I've met someone new. It's all been a bit of a rush, but I do know that I have never been happier. He will be here any minute.'

'Janice, it's all rather sudden, you mean you met someone while you were away? Have you done this to spite me?'

She smiled. 'Greg, don't do that to yourself. I feel no bitterness towards you. I need this job here, amongst these people, who seem to care for me, just as I care for them. I don't want to leave, and I don't want there to be bad feeling about something that now lies in the past. Riccardo loves me for who I am. He does not seem to mind *what* I am. He will be here any second and please say *hello*. He does not know about you and me, and I will not be telling him that we once had a fling that we both regretted in the cold light of day. No more needs to be said, does it?'

Greg's mouth opened but no words were produced. How much she'd changed in a few weeks. He could only nod.

It was true that, after the upset and despair of her hurried departure, she thought that she hated the young GP but realised that his stance on things was one to be pitied not despised. Ultimately, she understood that he was very much the victim of a rigid upbringing that left him little room for his own wishes. She knew that what she thought they'd shared was illusory, having learned much in a few short weeks. Initially, she'd cried a million tears. Her mother thought that she would never recover. On holiday she hadn't come out of her room for the first twenty-four hours. However, that second day, her mum had detected the handsome young man struggling with the beautiful Italian sports car, in the rain, as she looked out from the hotel window. Simply expressing sympathy for the young Italian and indicating the umbrella that was placed there, for the use of guests was enough to galvanise Janice into life-changing action. The two had been

162

inseparable after that day: Janice hardly being seen for the rest of their vacation until the day when they were due to fly home. Janice had presented Riccardo, and asked if she could travel with him back to England. Her dad shook the Italian's hand and her mum didn't seem able to resist the urge to throw her arms around his slim neck.

Janice stood, recognising that Dr Stevens had nothing else to say. The compelling smile, now so much in force on her pretty face. She shook his hand as if now marking the limits of the relationship that would exist between them in the future.

Just as she turned to go, he saw the beautiful engagement ring on her left hand. He then, in that moment, understood the reason for the excited, almost breathless, smile and the sparkle in her eyes. He understood, too, the meaning of regret and of foolish miscalculation. She left the room without looking back. The others in reception had noticed the wonderful two-carat flawless diamond solitaire set in Platinum. Heads turned towards the entrance. A tall, slim young man with sandy-brown hair and Mediterranean skin had just walked in. His hazel eyes, with tiny blue flecks that sparkled as a reflection of Janice's, scanned the room, searching for the person who then rushed over. In that moment, each person understood the reason for her ecstatic happiness. The other receptionists stood open-mouthed. One asked him if he had a brother. Janice held his hand and tugged excitedly at one of his long arms.

'Everyone, please say hello to the man of my dreams. This is Riccardo.' She held up the ring so that everyone could get a better look. Matt was absolutely delighted for the young woman, his mood already in the ascendant because of the clues she'd uncovered. He rushed over to her, hugged and kissed her, just before shaking the young Italian's hand.

'Riccardo *you*,' he offered with a slight emphasis, 'are a lucky man.'

'I know that, Doctor Sinclair. I am so pleased to meet you. Janice has told me a lot about you.'

'Well, she's told us nothing about you, so I'm guessing that this is all rather new.'

'Yes my car had broken down. I was stranded by the side of the road. Dark rain clouds were gathering overhead. Suddenly I looked up and Janice here, she had rushed out of her hotel, on the north shore of Lake Como, to help me. I was quite taken, as you say, with her. I looked up and there she was like a guardian angel come to watch over me. Complete with large umbrella, under which we both sheltered. I wined and dined her every night until I persuaded her to say *yes* and here we are. A bit of a whirlwind romance, as you say.'

'So, will you be relocating to the UK?'

'My father has an engineering works in Turin. We supply Fiat and of course Ferrari.'

Matt's eyes widened. There was something about how a native speaker pronounced this most iconic of Italian motor vehicles.

'I hoped she would come and live with me in Bellagio, but she says she couldn't possibly leave her friends here. So, it looks as though you'll be seeing much more of me.'

Matt's eyes widened again, swallowing hard, almost shocked by the news, but delighted to be seeing the two together, blushing with new found love in his reception. Fabienne too came over to hug Janice and to kiss Riccardo. Both she and Matt noticed the way he stared at Janice as though she were the only person in the room. Such sentiments each knew from their own experiences. Fabienne nodded gently to Matt as she caught his eye and smiled.

The unspoken communication conveyed between them very much one of mutual approval.

Eventually, Greg joined the party, and though there was a slight gap in the conversation as he entered, Janice moved quickly to grab his arm and to present him to her fiancé.

'Dr Stevens, please meet Riccardo who, after much pleading, I have agreed to marry,' offered Janice, still with that sense of ecstasy in her voice.

Greg's deep rich, velvety voice had a slight crick in its tone. Greg looked keenly at the tall, slim young man as they shook hands. He couldn't help but wonder if Janice had told the truth, or if, as with so many, she couldn't resist the temptation to mention their previous liaison. He knew that most young people would have spilled the beans at the outset. He could see, however, as he looked keenly at Riccardo, that there was absolutely no trace of pre-existing knowledge, no searching looks, no pauses, no questions on his open expression. It then became obvious that the young Italian had not been burdened in this way as he met Greg for the very first time. In that moment he couldn't help but admire Janice just a little bit more - and himself just a little less.

None of this interaction was lost on Matt, as he glanced once again at his wife who returned the enigmatic flash from her understanding smile as the same thoughts crossed both minds simultaneously. How much the young woman had grown, and how mature she had become in such a short space of time. Regrets, if there were any at all present in that room that day, lay firmly within the young GP, who knew in that moment he'd struggle to find someone like Janice. He saw there and then all the factors that made her so special: her warmth, her kindness, the sheer excitement that seemed to exist in each breath she took. To this list he now found himself adding discretion and wisdom – surely, he considered, pretty rare attributes in today's world.

Fabienne detected the slight pause running on Greg's face and moved forward quickly.

'Cake, Riccardo?' offered Fabienne.

Riccardo patted his slim, rippled stomach, as if this would be an incautious thing to take, but after a reassuring nod from Janice decided to eat. Matt looked on, doing his best to hide the sense of horror from appearing on his visage. Riccardo chose a large slice of coffee-and-walnut cake that Matt considered at least looked safe to eat. Unfortunately he'd been caught out on more times than he'd wish to consider.

The words that Fabienne had waited to hear all her life then came forth.

'Miss Fabienne, I see that you are as good a cook as you are a singer.' Riccardo looked on with sheer delight, as he continued to chew.

Matt couldn't help wondering if he'd have employed such words six months before Mary's intervention. He looked at Fabienne and caught her looking back just before he was able to mask the utter admiration and affection he held for her. She smiled again, with only a slight raise in one of her eyebrows giving any indication that she'd detected some of his earlier thoughts.

'Please call me, Sylvie, Riccardo, as all my friends do,' she suggested, while the relaxed smile was transferred once again from the young man, who was despatching the piece of cake with a speed, which underlined the sincerity of his compliment, to her husband who winked back.

Stars' End

CHAPTER XVI

HEAVEN'S GATE

Matt dared to hope that events were now behind he and his wife, things settling down quite quickly within days of his reinstatement. Once again, the news flow turned positive: Fabienne's agent phoned a few days later with the news that she'd been offered a part in a film that was being shot at Pinewood studios from the following spring. They wanted her to go and do an audition the following week. Though this had been mooted before, the offer was hastily withdrawn when the news about Barry Miles hit the newsstands and her stock plummeted to an all time low. As Christmas approached, Matt quickly got back into his pattern of work, and both he and his patients were delighted that this was so. Fabienne's instinct about him needing his work, his patients and his surgery had been proven correct with a graphic and brutal demonstration when all this had seemed to be in doubt. Mr Foster had not been in contact, but Matt heard that he had managed to salvage his career, if not his promotion, by pursuing Dr Letworth. Jim Duggan had been fired once again by the *Daily Scorcher* and was now facing charges, along with the suspended female GP, of conspiracy to commit fraud. Though Matt had been informed of the new events, he did his best to keep them at the periphery of his consciousness, detecting that it was most definitely time to move on. He accepted that harbouring bitterness and regrets would sabotage this process.

One lunchtime, just before Christmas, Matt was quietly watching the news with Fabienne sitting next to him. The phone rang and Fabienne answered.

'Can I speak to Matt?' Were the only words conveyed, but Fabienne instantly recognised Rita's voice. Her ears tuned as sensitively as her nostrils.

'Just a moment please.'

She handed him the handset and voiced the word 'Rita' to him, as she motioned that she would leave the room. She had packing to do for she was leaving the next day for a concert in Sydney. She'd promised Matt that she would be back in good time for Christmas and they were hoping to spend it together. He held her wrist gently and patted the sofa next to him.

'Rita, what can I do for you?'

'Matt, please forgive me. I am so sorry. I must have been out of my mind to try to hurt you in this way.'

'It's all in the past now, Rita,' he offered reassuringly, but Fabienne desperately fought down other emotions while her eyes glanced towards the ceiling with frustration.

'I need to see you, Matt, to apologise in person. Are you between surgeries now? I thought you could maybe pop round?'

'No, that isn't necessary, Rita. It's all over now, and I am not going to start bearing grudges. Let's both move on shall we?'

'Please Matt, let me see you one more time, and you won't hear from me again.'

Matt knew that the CPS was now building a case against both she and Jim Duggan, and this was perhaps quite correct. He'd heard that her partners had moved to eject her from the partnership and also that Jim Duggan was once again jobless.

'Very well then Rita, I'll be right over before I start my afternoon surgery.

Fabienne shook her head in a resigned fashion; she knew this was the way with her husband, but she loved him for it, and therefore did her best to hide her lack of enthusiasm both for Dr Letworth and the request she'd made.

He dabbed the handset to terminate the call, and turned to his wife. 'Is it ok if I pop over there? Do you want to come with me?'

'No thanks, Matt, I realise this is something you need to do, and if that's the case, then please do it, finish this thing, and perhaps then we can get on with our lives?'

Sensing her unease despite her absolute trust in his motives, he kissed her hand. 'I'll be right back. It shouldn't take long to hear her out.'

'Ok then. I'll get the coffee on so don't be gone long. I'll be polishing my Australian accent.'

'Yes, could do with a bit of work from what I remember!' he said, both remembering the day they'd spent in the leisure centre and Matt had introduced her as his cousin from Melbourne.

He kissed her again, grabbed his jacket, and walked slowly out to his car.

Some minutes later the phone rang again and Fabienne answered, detecting Steve's voice. 'Hi, Steve. Matt? No, you've just missed him by about 5 minutes. He's gone to Rita's. She phoned him and asked him to pop round. You know what he's like, said it wasn't necessary but she insisted on meeting face-to-face. I am not sure it's a good idea, but if it helps him move on and put it all behind him, then I thought why not.'

The simplicity, but incredulous tone, of Steve's words raised more of an alarm within as she detected panic now rising.

'What, Sylvie? And you let him go!'

'He seemed keen to finish it so I told him to go and do that so we could put it all behind us.'

Steve's brilliance as a psychologist was matched only by his instinct. He'd built a career on teasing the important from the unimportant; from looking into the minds of men and women; finding the little fragments of information; holding the key to the puzzle that would often set a patient on the road to recovery.

'I should have known she'd do something like this,' he said more to himself than Fabienne.

Fabienne was even more alarmed as he thought aloud, detected the concern rising in his voice.

His voice slowed even further than its usual laconic style. 'I don't think Rita is very well at the moment, Sylvie.' He recalled the conversation they'd had about a patient a week or two ago and he'd invoked then his other skill of detecting when a patient was dangerously on the edge, as now. 'I don't think we should let him go on his own. Follow him, Sylvie. Please don't let him go alone. Take your mobile. Phone me when you get there - and be careful.'

Though no further words were said, she realised that Steve was worried about his friend, emotions that had been now irrefutably transferred to her.

Fabienne flew from the house. She closed but didn't bother to lock their front door, racing over the gravel, which gave a staccato crunching noise with the rapidity of her steps. The R8 started immediately with a throaty growl while the transmission engaged the steering mounted paddles. Quadruple exhausts soon vented the magnificent engine as it flew down the drive, gravel fragments flying up as the wide tyres bit into them for purchase.

Rita met Matt at the front door. She'd clearly been looking out for his arrival. She closed the door firmly behind him, and led

171

the way through the house. He had visited once, briefly, some years before. She sat him in the front reception room, the sumptuous chairs, overlooking the manicured lawns, and the wall of folding glass doors that looked out onto the patio. Expensive fabrics framed the expanse.

'Sit down Matt. Thank you for coming. I won't be a minute, I'll just get a drink.'

He sat in the large armchair just facing the large windows.

She presented with a large metal tray and placed it on a small table in front of the great windows. Complete with two aluminium chairs, it looked completely out of place as if it had been usually situated on the patio outside and not in the house.

'No, not there, Matt. Sit facing me here.'

She indicated the seat facing, and Matt got up from the comfortable armchair. Sitting awkwardly in the aluminium one, which groaned uneasily under his weight, Matt did as he was asked. His long bony legs poked forwards under the small table. She pushed the stainless steel tray towards him. She was staring intently at him and all his attention was focused on her. He paid little attention to the tray - until it was too late. He realised then in an instant how gullible, how foolish he'd been - and now he was to pay the price.

Something was very wrong. Rita had a wild look in her eyes. He'd seen her shout at just about anyone, lose her temper, insult people and put them down with her razor-like mind. However, even at her most insulting, in the midst of her most fiery outbursts, he'd never seen her face generate such a look.

Matt saw the flash of a glass syringe, but far too late.

He knew straight away what must be in that syringe even as the sharp but burning pain hit his thigh. He tried to stand as the searing pain rushed through him and he realised that he had only seconds of consciousness left to him. He knew he would then be at the mercy of someone who was clearly intent on doing him harm. The drug hit him long before he could direct his legs to stand. By this time they were incapable of doing so.

She pushed him almost casually back into the metal-framed chair; a look of pure revenge now visiting her tortured features.

'Sit, down Matt, my darling, this will take but a minute, and will allow me to settle our last score.'

Producing a pair of dressmaker's shears, she proceeded to cut his clothing from him. This was the last thing he remembered as the contents of the syringe played upon his conscious state with devastating effect. He lost consciousness just as the blades of the scissors sliced through his clothing.

'Won't be long now Matt, my dear,' as she kissed him obsequiously, 'then we'll settle this once and for all. Her lush lips, with the brash red lipstick, were now pouting with expectation. Seems you'll be leaving us, I fear,' she said, patting his cheek, his eyes closed and his brain now dormant as his conscious state plummeted down the coma scale.

Fabienne sped through the village with unaccustomed urgency. The residents had seen her on many occasions guide the powerful and impactful car with infinite care as she negotiated the narrow confines of the village of Perrilymm. For some reason, however, things that day were to be different: she travelled down the cramped roads with as much speed as she thought her skills as a driver would allow. Observers thought this very strange, though the more observant would have noticed her car spend one or two nights on the pavement outside Jane Tomkins' little cottage, and the most observant of all would have even noted that Jane's little Honda Jazz had been missing throughout this time.

The pop star gripped the steering wheel with a force that reflected the panic inside and mirrored mounting fears as to exactly what was about to be visited on her husband. Reasonable people's minds ran with reasonable thoughts. It was hard but sometimes necessary to assume much more uncomfortable thoughts about the minds, the beliefs and intentions of others. Steve was normally so calm; she had detected the panic in his voice as soon as she had told him where Matt had gone. Just how could she have let him go? She realised in that moment that she should have stopped him: understanding that she'd never be able to live with the consequences if something happened to him.

Fabienne approached Rita's house, having covered the distance at a faster speed than she'd thought herself capable. In truth she realised that all other considerations were now in abeyance, including her own safety.

She crept round the back of the house.

Nothing could prepare her for the sight she was to witness through the windows. Matt was unconscious and completely naked. His limbs had been delicately wrapped with rolls of gauze dressings binding his 4 limbs to the arms and front legs of the metal chair. Fabienne could not understand why such bonds had been used and why he was naked.

Rita had prepared what looked like a drip stand, fashioned from an old clothes steamer. From the stand hung a little bag of clear, colourless fluid, in to which the end of a clear plastic tube had been pushed.

Matt was stirring as she was making her preparations. Fabienne pulled back a little in order to remain undetected. She phoned Steve, her shaking hands barely able to activate the screen. She wanted to gulp and to cry and to scream. His calming words were at their most entreating.

'Keep calm, Sylvie, I need you to tell me exactly what you can see. I am on my way, but I need you to help me so I can help him.'

'Okay, I can see he's strapped to a metal chair. He is naked and he's in danger, Steve.'

'Breathe slowly - try not to let the image distress you. What else can you see?'

'He has a strap round his left arm like a tourniquet they use when they take blood.'

'Good, now, what else can you see?'

'On the little table, there is a metal tray. It has on it a glass syringe like they used to use. I thought they used plastic syringes these days?'

'Yes they do. You clever girl.' Steve knew in that moment that the syringe contained Paraldehyde. This was used in days gone by to subdue violent patients. These days it was used to control unstable patients whose epilepsy was so bad that their bouts of fitting could not be stopped by any other means. He also knew that Rita had planned her attack on Matt with care and a lot of forethought. By selecting a glass syringe, she had created more of a window of opportunity to attack him. Paraldehyde, if retained in a plastic syringe for too long, would have dissolved it, so rendering it useless. She needed a glass one to give her more time.

Steve was now in a great rush. He knew, without doubt, that Matt was in extreme danger. Realising that it was more vital than ever that he remain calm, or that the poor woman would panic.

His surging thoughts and rising distress meant that he nearly didn't ask his next question.

'Fabienne, what else can you see?'

'She has some glass vials and a little bag of fluid, it looks like a drip with clear plastic tubing.'

175

Heaven's Gate

As Rita continued to work on the drip and its contents Matt stirred. 'Whoa big, boy won't be long now.' She jabbed the butterfly into a vein in his arm and taped it in, securely. To the socket coming from the butterfly she attached the plastic tubing.

'Rita what are you doing?'

'Look Matt, it was always meant to be this way. If you are interested, you suffered sudden cardiac arrest, whilst having rampant, swing-from-the-chandelier, sex with me. Who would think anything else about you? You've slept with the entire female staff of hospitals. I was just one amongst many, another notch on the bed post.'

'It wasn't like that Rita, we had something, but it was so long ago. We are different people now. Both you and I have moved on.'

'Too bad, handsome. I want the old Matt back, and if I can't have him then no one else can. I'll tell them how well you performed, don't you worry. I'll tell them that you suddenly grunted and groaned in sheer ecstasy, and then your heart stopped. That stupid, half-blind pathologist with the bottle-bottomed glasses at Mirfield general can hardly see. They'll never find the mark on your arm with that tiny needle and there won't be any marks from those bandages when I've unwrapped them and placed you. Sorry, that would, of course, be your cold lifeless body on the floor. I'll appear all traumatised, and so guilty in my little silk negligée when they get here.

That stupid trollop you married will never know what happened. She'll think you cheated on her for the very last time. Don't worry though, Matt, I'll tell her how good you were, like you used to be. Magnificent Matt, stallion man, went right through the afternoon, and then whoops - he died whilst having naughty nooky with me. Just like we used to have. I might even be able to

176

slip that fact in – though in-between my tears, of course. Make no mistake, Matt, it will be my finest performance. She'll see you in a different light once I have told my distressing tale. That should take the wind out of her sails a bit.'

An hysterical laugh was given off while she thought about the interviews she would give, the sorrow she would feign: no, the absolute shame she would convey for having been seduced by this man who said he simply just had to have her there and then, and no-one else was ever to know. He'd insisted that it was to be one last time. Such a cruel irony, his last words would remain forever for all to remember. She paused, for a moment: for she could see all this unfolding as if now gazing into the most detailed of images coming from a crystal ball.

'I'll have the last revenge on you Matt. Their enquiries into the study fiasco will be as nought when compared to your unsavoury, sordid little death here on my carpet. I'll drag your body onto the middle of my rug over there, a nice bottle of half-finished champagne, a few candles and some soft music, I think. I'll have my skimpiest slip on under the negligée, and I'll give them more than a glimpse of flesh like your whore of a wife did a couple of weeks ago. Little slut will never know what's hit her when I've finished. I should have phoned Jim to come and take some photos—perhaps it's not too late.' Once again the shriek of a laugh came forth as she tossed her head back and a row of strong white teeth appeared.

'Rita don't do this, we can still be friends.' He struggled violently but the layer upon layer of bandaged which overwrapped many times his ankles and his wrists was simply too strong.

'No, I think not, Matt dear, it's too late for us and it's now too late for you. Any last wishes?'

'Don't do this Rita, I'm begging you.'

'Funny, I seem to remember I was the one begging you to come and work in a proper surgery, but no, it wasn't good enough for goody two-shoes Sinclair and his whore of a wife.'

He shouted but there was no one to hear his cries - or so he believed.

Fabienne, was overawed and engulfed by distress in equal measure, to witness such a scene. She knew she had to remain calm; she could sense Steve, willing her to complete the assignment that he'd set her and then he'd come and help her, and Matt.

She continued to describe the scene to Steve. 'I can see some glass vials. Looks as though these have been broken and their contents put in the little bag.'

'What are they? Tell me, Sylvie, I need to know what's going in that drip?'

'Chloride, chloride!'

'No, that's not it. Is there anything else? Can you make anything else out?'

'Yes, it's Potassium Chloride.'

'Potassium Chloride!'

Steve froze, as the game plan was revealed to him in all its gruesome detail. His world ended in that moment, just as he knew Matt's was about to. A ghost crossed his grave in that instant: shivers progressed violently down his spine. He wanted to scream to the heavens that this could not be happening, but he knew only that he could no longer waste the final seconds of what would be his best friend's life. He wondered how he could possibly tell Mary that he was on the phone as Matt died. He remembered with even more horror that she was due to deliver today. He wondered if in future it would also commemorate Matt's death: a constant reminder of a friend who was no longer present.

Steve knew this deadly poison of old. It was the one most chosen by the medical profession- so popular among the medical fraternity; fast, brutal and deadly. This was invariably the quick, clean and irreversible exit that they chose. With mounting horror he realised that this was almost a bespoke drug used by medics to exit when things became too hard, exams had been failed, a serious court case was pending, a coroner's court or simply the depths of abject depression. He'd known several junior doctors who'd chosen to end their lives in this way.

The massive concentration of Potassium Chloride would stop a heart within seconds. Resuscitation was just about impossible. And should such cases come before pathologists, hunting for clues as to the sudden death of the recipient, it was all but untraceable. Unless the body was discovered complete with either a syringe or giving-set and drip. If such evidence were removed from the death-scene, no one would ever be able to distinguish the cause of death from a sudden unpredictable, unforeseen cardiac arrest that just about anyone could suffer at any time, given the conditions.

Steve responded quickly. He slowed his speech right down, but spoke clearly and concisely. He knew ultimately that she was the only hope.

The desperate side of him that had seen how quickly such a compound could work on the human heart, knew surely that it must already be way too late. Even now, Matt could be arresting.

'Sylvie, listen to me and listen now. I am on my way. There is an ambulance on its way. You have to get in there, you have to stop that drip, and you have to do it soon. Only you can save him. Forgive me; it's all up to you now.'

Heaven's Gate

Steve had no need to spell it out; Fabienne could tell from the delicate gaps in their conversation that he knew that Matt faced something that was merciless, quick and deadly.

Fabienne, in that moment, was compelled to think of all the terrifying episodes of her life. From an early age she'd witnessed violent rows between her parents, conducted with scant regard for the little girl who'd taken to stand between them in an attempt to insulate one another from the other's unremitting anger. The nights too that she covered her ears with her pillow in an attempt to drown out the shouting and the screaming between two people who were supposed to be the adults. More than once as she'd cried herself to sleep some hours after the disruption had subsided; she'd crept down the following morning to see if both had survived the night, now too terrified to peep round the kitchen door. Inevitably this brought thoughts back about other times she suffered with sheer terror coursing through her brain. The night she'd arrived home from a night out with friends, not knowing what awaited her in the darkness. She remembered the grim discovery in that moment of turning the light on in her bedroom. The night that Barry Miles had killed himself with a ligature round his neck as he'd pulled on that cord that swept around the pulley he'd attached to the door in order to asphyxiate himself for the sole purpose of pursuit of sexual gratification. She remembered the horror of seeing his lifeless, bloated and cyanosed body and the condition it was in when she'd discovered him. All her personal, most intimate things turned out of her drawers and strewn around the room.

Knowing that the person who'd saved her from that experience was dying behind that glass. She understood the way Steve had implored her, almost begging her to do something because he knew that no one else could. It didn't, therefore require

180

a massive leap of logic to recognise that her husband must be in extreme and imminent danger. Never having heard of Potassium Chloride was, in many ways irrelevant: she'd grasped that it must spell death, knowing Steve as she did - and detecting the realisation that came to him, which had been accompanied by sheer panic, though he'd done his best to shield her from such thoughts. She could see the feverish animated movement from Rita who had this odd look in her eye, as might someone who had suddenly discovered something that no one else could see.

Fabienne banged on the window. Rita turned round. 'Too late you effin cow, he's all mine and you can have his cold lifeless body when I am good and ready to let you have it—you'll never get in in time. It's all over for him and it's now all over for you. I hate you; I hate both of you. I hope you both rot in hell. Time to say goodbye, why not blow him your last kiss through this thickened glass?'

Fabienne realised she wasn't able to break the glass with her fists. She looked round desperately for a garden tool or a brick- anything that might be brought to bear.

She then tried the sliding door, but it was locked firmly. No doubt it was fitted with dead locks in order to keep burglars out.

Steve hurtled down to pharmacy. He banged on the counter with uncharacteristic vigour - they were about to close.

'I need some vials of rapid acting insulin—please.'

The pharmacist looked at him suspiciously. It was years since psychologists used insulin comas as a form of shock treatment for resistant depressed patients. These days ECT or electro- convulsive therapy was used. What could a psychologist possibly need insulin for?

'We're about to close, Dr Collins. Have you a prescription?'

'I need some dextrose infusion too—please.

'Very well. A *prescription*, please?' The pharmacist had slowed his speech down and emphasised the need for a prescription, as if trying to explain his dilemma to Steve.

'I need them now, this minute, please.' Dr Collins was habitually very polite. He was calm, measured, jovial and always relaxed. The pharmacist knew that, any minute now, up would come his arm and he would agree, with a cheery wave to return after lunch with the required prescription for an exchange, although he still could not think what a psychologist would want with such things. As he looked more carefully, the pharmacist recognised something of urgency, bordering on instability about him, almost as though he was up to something illicit— and he wondered if he had been working too hard.

'I'm going to need to see a prescription, Dr Collins.'

Steve blinked, then breathed in very quickly, he swallowed hard. 'I see, look it's like this. Hand it over now and quickly, otherwise you'll have someone's death on your hands, and it will be, all your fault. Long before that happens, however, I'll have jumped over this counter, and I'll have ripped your head off. Now get these items for me now—please! Or am I going to have to go nuclear?'

'I see Dr Collins, well, since you put it in those terms, here we are. And from the fridge some insulin. Is Apidra satisfactory?' He handed over vials of Apidra and also some bags of Dextrose infusion. The pharmacist felt shocked and more than a little numb. His mouth opened to speak, but no words would come. They always said that psychiatrists had the most stressful job, and no doubt it also applied to psychologists too.

Steve managed a 'thank you' just before he sped off down the corridor in order to look for his car. He was now praying that it

182

would start and he still had time to get there. This would without doubt depend entirely on Fabienne and whether or not she had gained entry. If not, then he might as well take his time: it would be just about all over for his friend whose silent, lifeless shell would be the only thing left of him once his heart stopped and his brain ceased.

Fabienne's thoughts were moving still more quickly. She calmly slipped her mobile in her back pocket. Rita saw her step away from the window. 'That's right, clear off you stupid bitch; it's too late to save him now anyway.' She re-directed her attention to the task in hand. The drip went up.

Matt could only offer a 'Don't do this Rita,' he then desperately tried to reach the drip with his mouth to pull it clear, but she had taped it back up along his arm and out of his reach. He knew finally that his pleas were a waste of breath - breath that was now in short supply: for his life would rapidly slip away as an elegant but brutal poison would soon be at work. He realised, too, that the part of Rita he used to know had been subsumed by something a lot less healthy, and she was now unequivocally controlled by the paranoid illness that resided within.

Perhaps he should have detected the signs a long time ago. Perhaps he should have known that she would snap in this way. A coiled spring that would sweep aside everything that lay in its path, with no force available that would be able to stop it.

Suddenly, an almighty crash came through the patio doors as the panes dissolved into a million fragments. Fabienne had picked up one of the stone planters, full of plants, on the patio and thrown it—straight through the glass. The heavy object cracked a floorboard as it skidded to a halt behind Matt's chair.

The drip continued to run. Initially Rita was stunned with the violence of Fabienne's entry. Jumping through the shattered frame, she lunged for the tube. Rita, however, quickly recovered and anticipated this move. She grabbed the steel tray, initially like a shield. With her other hand she located another glass syringe from the tray, holding it like a dart. With the flat metal tray, she tried to swat Fabienne. As Rita advanced she adopted a slight crouched position, like a panther about to leap. The tray was used to make violent sweeping movements in front of Fabienne. Her other hand made stabbing thrusts with the loaded syringe. 'You can join him, you stupid whore. It won't take a minute. I've got enough for the two of you.' Fabienne parried the thrust from the tray with her left arm. The tray gave off a loud 'thwack' as it abutted against the pop star's forearm. Fabienne registered no pain as the force buckled the tray. Initially, she crept backwards but then quickly spun round, grabbing the other aluminium chair as she did so.

Matt had seen first-hand how she was able to execute complex dance moves, how she was able to sing and to dance almost without taking breath. He'd seen her up close, too, at the leisure pool when swimming, just how fit and how fast she was. Rita was surprised by her agility, her strength and, above all, her speed. Had she been to one of Fabienne's concerts, she would have seen like thousands of others that the performance she gave was very much that of an athlete as well as a singer.

This was to pale into insignificance now with the forces that panic had unleashed within. The gaze from the blue crystal eyes, now turning to solid ice as Fabienne mounted her offensive.

She used the chair, as would a lion tamer. First to knock the syringe from Rita's grasp with an almost surgical swipe from just one of the chair's legs and then advanced forwards, pushing her between its legs. As she spun round again, placing her back to Matt, her left leg came up with a sweeping movement behind her in order to knock the drip-stand down.

She continued to push forwards, turning round for the briefest moment as she looked at Matt. 'Hang on darling. I'll be with you in just a moment. You aren't cold are you, with that window and all?'

'Sylvie—look!' Matt implored her.

Rita had used Fabienne's distraction to sidestep the advancing chair, and was about to lunge towards Matt.

Fabienne quickly flipped the chair, so that she was now holding two of the legs and used the backrest to sweep sideways into the female GPs midriff winding her in the process.

'You've done this before.' Matt offered.

'The number of fights I saw my Mum and Dad get into, you'd better believe it.'

The blow was enough to cause Rita to drop the tray. She quickly crumpled, clutching her stomach. Fabienne held the chair to one side while her leg came up to push her adversary to the ground in the direction of the large, heavy rug.

'Remind me never to pick an argument with you, won't you.'

'Every day, my darling,' she responded, once again turning to Matt. 'I'll get you an overcoat or something in a minute.'

'Watch her,' he shouted, as Rita hit the rug still writhing in pain. 'Don't watch me!'

With blistering speed, no manoeuvre could be executed more quickly; Fabienne then lifted the edge of the wool rug and began rolling it towards Rita's prostrate form. The female GP was struggling now, not only to breathe but also to compass just what had hit her. Fabienne continued to roll the rug, like an avalanche down a hillside, with Rita imprisoned inside, its weight meaning that she would be unable to move. Fabienne placed the chair over the rug to stop Rita from rolling out, smacked her palms together as if the movements had all been rehearsed, and turned to Matt with something of satisfaction. 'Do you think the old cow will be able to breathe in there?'

'I expect so.'

'Pity.'

'That's not like you, my love.'

'She's lucky I saw the rug!' she concluded, still barely out of breath. She continued, 'Well, Matt, my love, that was exciting. Can I ask you just what do you do to all these women?'

'I wish I knew.'

Fabienne could hear the ambulance sirens in the distance.

Steve was also driving as fast as his ageing Ford Mondeo would convey him. He looked at the bags of Dextrose and the vials of insulin on the seat. He could only hope that Fabienne had managed to gain entry, as he knew otherwise both he and the ambulance would be too late.

He didn't have time to phone Fabienne, although he reasoned that, in any case, if things had gone according to plan, as he dared to hope, she would have been too busy to speak to him. It was perhaps a measure of how much danger he understood his friend to be in: for he could not help but think back to a low point in their relationship. He thought how well his friend had done; how, despite all the odds, Matt had followed a hunch to meet up with the girl of his dreams. The GP would, of course, say that his feelings had been so strong that he could not have done otherwise. Steve then remembered the tirade of criticism that he'd placed at his friend's door when he'd announced that, far from expunging the rock star from his life, he'd planned to meet up with her.
186

Worse than all these thoughts, however, as was the way, was not the present but the absent. This, of course, was an apology, which was long overdue. He promised himself, that if Matt came through this, then immediately after congratulating him on his deliverance would come an abject apology.

'Matt, lets get you free from the chair and get you decent.' Fabienne moved towards him while she went about releasing his bonds. She could hear Rita's muffled cries from inside the rolled up rug. 'You stay there, you randy cow. He's spoken for, and you had your chance ten years ago. He's all mine, and you can't have him, even if you do rip all his clothes off.'

Rita went quiet.

'So, as I was saying before we were rudely interrupted, just what do you do to them all?'

'I just wish I knew,' was all he could offer.

When asked later, she could not say why she had decided to start unwrapping the bandages that bound Matt's legs rather than disconnect the drip, the butterfly needle remaining in his arm vein, blood now flowing backwards along the tube towards the small bag of saline that Rita had laced with deadly Potassium Chloride.

Matt looked at the little infusion bag on the floor and thought how lucky he'd been; his wife's speed of reaction and agility had saved him. Only then did he see that the bag was empty. He caught her eye, just as she looked at him.

She followed his line of sight and saw that the bag was empty. The contents had run through completely. She stared, open-mouthed with sheer horror, there was no time for speech. Time had run out, along with the little bag of saline. The deadly payload was on its way.

'Sylvie,' was the last word he spoke.

Heaven's Gate

Fabienne looked at him. She noticed the colour drain from him in an instant. At first his heart gave but the briefest of shimmers, the so-called ventricular fibrillation, followed by an agonal rhythm that could provide no output. It was all an academic point in any case: his heart stopped in that moment. Doctors might talk of 'complete asystole', which was a technical word for a lifeless heart - as silent, now, as the death that came to claim him. The heart that had been beating for 28 years, its electrical rhythm, stopped in as many seconds, by toxic levels of potassium.

He slumped forward in the chair, his breathing having stopped some moments before.

Death came upon him in that instant, almost as quickly as Fabienne could scream.

Angels came tumbling from the heavens in a silent but wondrous cascade. He, of course, was the first to see them, gazing spellbound by the magnificent sight. He pointed and shouted, but then realised that he was incapable of pointing, shouting or showing others what he, alone, could see.

At first he was aware of the loud sirens, the violent banging on the front door, but then things became quiet. The sirens and the splintering of the front doorframe were the last things he heard. Absolute quiet, with no birds in the branches or rustle of the wind; not even the sound of breathing, or the sobs of despair. A bright light descended and appeared to be directed towards him. Time disengaged: he was now heading for a place where time was irrelevant since it had never begun and therefore had no end. He looked back with some pain: the young woman pressing furiously on his chest, but she had spent too long on trying to give him mouth to mouth. The compressions when they came were too high up his breastbone to provide any output at all from a heart that had ceased to beat. In any event the potassium levels were firmly in the lethal range. She looked up and he saw her mouth open to emit a scream that he could no longer hear. He wondered if she had looked straight at him in that moment as she wept and her own heart shrieked with despair. He thought for an instant about the pain and about the loss, but the angels assured him he was heading for a place with none of these things where he could remain forever. Stars appeared at that juncture, but then went out one by one. As the stars ended, he sensed that he was now journeying to a place that had neither given birth to them, nor needed them to sustain it.

The light grew brighter. At first it hurt his eyes, but he realised that hurt and pain had gone and was left behind. The light advanced, it seemed to now be above him and drawing him upwards, enveloping him as it did so. He glanced backwards just the once. He could see a man's lifeless body, which suddenly jerked, and he realised that it would not move again. In addition, others continued to flood into the room as the woman was carefully prised from the dead body. It all seemed so far away, separated now by so much more than distance: that was another place, another time and another existence. He looked up, the angels touched him gently, and he followed without looking back.

CHAPTER XVII

OF DEATH AND LIFE - STARS ETERNAL

Long fingers tapped her hips briskly. Not even the absolute black of the Kenyan night could disguise her impatience. She looked down from the balcony, desperately trying to pierce the all-enveloping darkness, which now immersed her.

Only the stars accompanied her now. She knew, without looking up, that they were there: for she understood that they would never end—unlike flesh and blood, and of course, tears. A shiver ran down her spine while she stood alone, the scintillating umbrella of stars only a glance away. She resisted the urge to engage with their magnificence and their majesty, whilst unquantifiable flares of pure energy were consumed at what must surely be as close to infinity as made no difference.

'Please come out here,' she paused, expectantly.

'I need you to see this,' as she tried again.

'I can't look up until you are here,' voicing a further appeal.

'This will amaze you!' making her final attempt.

'I can't,' came from the male voice from inside the lodge.

'Why?'

'I'm busy.'

'You're busy?' She sighed, once again, as she summoned more reserves of patience.

'With what, may I ask?'

'I'm reading the newspaper.' She laughed as she heard these words arrive from the interior of the lodge, which was completely dark.

'There aren't any newspapers out here. We're in the middle of most deserted Kenya. Perhaps I should say darkest, deserted Kenya. So, I'm guessing that it's too dark in there to see, let alone read. And, you may wish to know, it's just like that out here.'

'I'm going to put on the light,' came from the male voice that was now laden with more mischief.

'Don't you dare! I have it on good authority from a doctor, I once knew, that if you do that, our eyes will take ages getting used to the dark again.'

'These doctors don't know what they are talking about.'

'Come out here and see this wonderful night. I'm begging you.'

'I can't.'

'Just why not?'

'It's bad for my arthritis.'

'But you haven't *got* arthritis,' her voice now going up a semitone with exasperation.

'I might have, if I step out there.'

'You'll have a sore bottom, if you don't step out here. I should warn you: I am wearing particularly pointy shoes.'

The male voice burst into a laugh. 'I didn't see you wearing those on our trek this afternoon?'

'No, I put them on only when I'm negotiating—or more likely pleading. Now, come on, I am *begging* here. Besides my knees will get sore and my pointy shoes all scuffed, with this grovelling I'm doing.'

'You did say pointy shoes?' came from the voice inside.

191

'Men! Tell me, is that *all* you think about?'

'I'm not coming out there, until you tell me that you love me.'

She smiled to herself and nodded, as understanding finally broke through her frustration. 'Not *that* again. I thought we'd settled that.'

Silence ensued. She continued, 'Okay, you come out here, and in return, much more than tell you - I'll *prove* that I love you.' She waited, holding her breath, as silence was the only thing now falling on her consciousness from the dark interior of the lodge. 'Now come on, I've been waiting for you for so long that the sun will be up soon.'

'That is an exaggeration, Miss Fabienne, I've only been reading for five minutes.'

With this, however, she heard a creak from the boards as he began moving towards her.

He appeared on the balcony and her hands were transferred from her own hips to enwrap his waist as she pulled him closer. Her grip reflecting her adamance that he was not, now, going to escape her.

'Now, look up and tell me what you see.' She looked up, in that moment, giving an involuntary gasp as the panorama of the limitless cosmos stretched before her.

'Nothing, absolutely nothing.'

'That is strange because I can see a billion stars.' The perfect blackness was punctuated by the pin-pricks of countless stars; some giving the illusion of flickering, almost as if light itself was unable to convey their unimaginable power.

'Now, where were we? Ahh yes, you were going to tell me that you loved me.' He reminded her.

192

'You know that doesn't mean a thing, don't you?'

'No? Really, can that be true?'

'Trust me. It's a lot of old hat. It doesn't stop people disappearing. It doesn't stop them losing their loved ones. It doesn't stop people from dying. Surely, it's just something people say, or think they should say. It's like a trendy word that people use for everything and in all circumstances.'

'I can't agree. I need to hear it, and I need to hear it from you.'

'You know, I'm certain, I've told you a hundred times. It didn't stop my mum and dad from destroying each other, as their love turned to hate.'

'That'll never happen.'

'Why, so?'

'It'll never happen, if you can only tell me what I need to hear.'

'I thought you men weren't interested in such things. I thought it was only we soppy females?'

'Don't believe all you hear. It'll be our secret, so don't let on I told you.'

'Well then,' she concluded, and at that juncture, almost as an afterthought, came words that he'd been expecting. 'One thing first?' She asked, as he felt her excitement grow, as her breathing sped up.

'Oh, oh, and what might that be?' He knew he had to ask, though little was needed by way of confirmation.

'You know.'

'No, I do not.'

'Tell me again?'

'Tell you what?'

Despite the all-embracing power of night, she could sense the smile rising on his face.

'Not *that* again.'

'Okay, we'll have a deal. You tell me what I want to know, and I'll tell you what you most want to hear.'

She sensed the slight delay, as he was unsure of whether or not to tease her for just a little while longer. She'd learned his ways by now, and knew that it was only a matter of time. She inhaled slowly while she waited. In any event she wasn't going to let him go until he told her.

This was the unabridged power of undiluted night. By having insufficient levels of light to be able to see, one relied more heavily on other senses, like hearing and touch. Each of the two people had become adept at reading what these other senses revealed to them.

'You don't want to know about the CDs do you?'

'No, not this time,' she said as he felt her head shake just a little from side to side.

'About my new surgery roof, then?'

'No, not that. *Definitely* not that!' He now felt the head shake more vigorously and the mouth move to suppress a rapidly forming swear word.

'It's quite interesting, you know. I could tell you all about those little tiny tiles they used.'

'Matt Sinclair! I am waiting,' he could feel her hands tense just a little more.

'Very well then, you want to know about Steve, don't you?' It was his turn to form an understanding and acquiescing nod.

'Yes, about Steve: you know what I want to hear.' He felt her head now nod, enthusiastically.

194

'Very well then, as you insist.' He hugged her; she was now so close that even his whispers seemed louder than the roars and bellows from deep in the Kenyan bush.

'Steve kicked the front door in, just as the paramedics got there. I have no idea how he managed to break through such a heavy door, but in he came.'

She licked her lips with anticipation; she could only hope that he'd tell his compelling tale slowly, so she could interrupt him at the exciting bits.

'He knew - and I don't know how he remembered, because he's not done any real medicine for years. It's a good job he used to study with me!'

'Show off!'

'Sorry. Shall I go on?'

'I think you'd better.'

'Now, where was I? Well, he knew that with that amount of potassium in my blood; even a shock from the defibrillator would not start it.'

'Yes, go on, I'm listening.'

'So, he used the insulin to force the potassium into the body's cells and away from the heart muscle. But, remember, if you do *just* that, you still kill your patient, because they die of low sugar. Many a person has been brought back, but in a vegetative state because the low sugar destroys their brain. Fortunately for my little grey cells, Steve knew that you have to give sugar, dextrose, via a drip. This keeps the sugar up while the insulin goes to work, bringing the potassium levels down.

'Go on, so how did he know that?'

'He knew that, because he's brilliant.'

'Are you sure?'

'Well, yes, I suppose so.'

'Is he as brilliant as you?'

'I suspect he might be.'

'And *he's* not conceited,' she said, placing her emphasis deliberately and tantalisingly.

'And you? Would you have done that?'

'Well, I was right out of it. So I couldn't possibly comment.'

'Too right. Anyway, go on, I am still listening.'

'Well, with the insulin being run in; the paramedics then had to compress the heart right here at the lower end of the breastbone.'

She felt him point to her breastbone. 'Not where I pushed then?'

'Sylvie, you did really well.'

'But just not at the right place.'

'You did your utmost. If it hadn't been for you, Rita would have stabbed them with that glass syringe.'

He felt her relax, just a little.

'Anyway, they pushed here to get the circulation flowing again. To try and get some output by compressing the heart chambers. Only then, as the potassium levels fell, could they then shock the heart with the defibrillator and so restart my heart. If the potassium had still been too high, my heart would not have restarted. At least that's the theory.'

'One mercifully, that was correct. So what was it like?'

'What?'

'Your out-of-body experience.'

'Oh that.'

'Yes?'

She knew they'd reached the touchy-feely stuff that he felt uncomfortable with, as did most men. She needed to know: for

196

this was the best bit. She'd spent days just getting to this point, and on each of these occasions he'd distracted her with other things. This time she was not going to be diverted. He felt her grip him even more tightly.

He knew that she just had to know, and that he could keep it from her no longer.

'Go on,' she said as he felt the sharp intake of breath that she'd taken.

'So, did I miss much?' he queried.

'Actually, quite a bit, Matt, especially the scary bits.'

'The scary bits. I hate the scary bits; I always hide behind a cushion when the scary bits come on.'

'Matt, that was a good idea, as this was particularly scary. So, where were we? Ah yes, you were about to tell me, before you changed the subject.' She paused, but couldn't stop the excited gaze, like a little girl on gazing through the pet shop window— mercifully that it was too dark for him to see. 'Was it wonderful?' she prompted.

'No, it was terrible.'

'How so?' If the light levels had been any higher, he would have seen shock appear on her face, her eyes narrowing as she tried to scrutinise him, in order to sense whether he was trying to tease her again.

'I nearly forgot about you.'

'Is that possible?'

'No, I don't think it is,' as if in that second, he realised a universal truth, similar to the forces that neutron stars, in their passionate and time-defying embrace, maintained long after the collapsing star, that had created them, had faded. 'At least, not for more than a millionth of a second,' he assured her.

'So, go on then. What was it like?'

'There was a quiet, and a peace, and a serenity about it. I saw an all-pervading bright light, and felt my body floating upwards. I was at peace, no pain, no suffering; just sheer bliss.'

'So, what stopped you? Were you not tempted to go?'

'No.'

'Why was that?'

'There was, no you.'

'But, surely with all that sheer bliss around?'

'It was the sight of you sobbing.'

'Are you sure, perhaps it was simply Steve's drugs?'

'No, absolutely not. I could see it as clear as day.'

'But, he is the one who saved you…'

'No, someone else saved me.'

'Who is that, was it the angels?'

'No, not even them.'

'The paramedics, then?'

'Not quite.'

She usually enjoyed the bits that he added each time he told his tale. A tale of which she would never tire - even if he were to tell it every day for the rest of their lives. She was certainly hoping this would be the case. She realised, however, that there had been one snippet, either that she'd missed or, more likely, that he'd not told her.

Her eyes widened still further, anticipation now flowing with excitement and impatience.

'Well, who then?'

'*You*, you saved me.'

'But, I did nothing apart from roll Rita in that big rug! It was a bit like a French farce.'

'A French farce?'

'You know, like the slapstick, you used to see on stage shows?'

'Oh yes I see, that's before my time.'

'I'm only going off what my granny told me, you *are* older than me, you know?' She paused, took another deep breath, and continued. 'So, how did I save you? You told me that I didn't even press on the right bit?' She just had to return to that little morsel that he'd revealed, just as was his wont each time the story was told, something new appeared.

'That was brilliant by the way, wrapping her in that rug.'

'Horny cow, I should have thrown her in a bath of cold water. Anyway, stop distracting me, and please continue. You were saying?'

'You saved me because of a decision you made in a split second. You unwrapped those bandages, *but* you left the drip in. For most people, this would have been the first thing they'd have pulled out.

Brilliant though Steve was, neither he nor the paramedics would have been able to get that line back in, with me collapsed on the floor. They simply wouldn't have had enough time. *You*, in that tiny move, saved me, and Miss Fabienne, since you asked, since you needed to know, I am going to remind you of that each time you ask me to tell my story.'

'Oh, I won't ask you again - I'm getting bored with it now,' she smiled, sensing that it was now her turn to start teasing him.

'That's not what you said this morning, and this afternoon, and last night, and on the flight over here,' he offered with dejection creeping into his voice. 'So does that mean, I can tell you about my surgery roof?'

'You do that, and I will divorce you. That paramedic who asked me to sign an autograph for his little girl wasn't half hunky, you know.'

'I can't say I noticed. Good job I'm not the jealous type.'

'No, I know that Matt Sinclair. I want to tell *you* something, now.'

'Now then. Look up,' she said, as he felt her neck extend. She continued, 'Just what do you see?'

'Nothing.'

'Well then, can you see that bright star over there, and that one?'

'Yes, now that you mention it.'

'You see, you're getting the hang of it now. I understand, so they tell me, that ever since my day on that little footbridge outside your, outside *our* house, that I have been looking up—that there are more than a billion stars up there.' She paused for a sharp intake of breath: here it was - what he most wanted to hear.

'You know, Matt Sinclair, that I loved you before the first of those stars was born, and I'll go on loving you until the very last of them has faded, and turned into a lump of charcoal no bigger than a boiled egg; or whatever stars do when they stop twinkling. You said that you'd crossed time for me. Well, I know that I was waiting, lost in time, for you to appear and set me free. That very first day, as soon as I'd swept the hat from my head. I knew that it was you. You suspended my belief in loneliness as being the only way to avoid the pain that I'd seen two people, who were once lovers, inflict on one another. You taught me with that single, awe-struck smile, that it was time to trust; that it could be done. And you were the man to do it. Even more importantly, you showed me what love means. What *true* love means. I sent that cheque back to you - not *Lucy*. I wanted to touch something that you would then touch.

You know, don't you Matt, that you saved me, long before Barry Miles sneaked into my bedroom and way, way, before Sheila Coombs try to petrol-bomb me. They also tell me that it's a very long interval of time before the first of those stars started flickering and it will be an even longer time until the last one goes out. However, regardless of what the stars do, I am going to remind you of all that, and kiss you like this.'

Life and dreams fused as one: she kissed him with a pent-up passion that only the endless Universe could contain. She kissed him until his heart quietened, and his head became fuzzy, and even then, she continued to kiss him.

At that moment light from a supernova, as the core of a massive star imploded, reached Earth following its kilo parsec journey, travelling for more than three-thousand light years since it began. The burst of radiation given off, exceeded the brightness of the sun over its entire lifespan, seemed to illuminate them as darkness was expunged.

He held her and whispered to her that he had always known that. He was sorry if he ever given her the impression otherwise. He knew as the years passed that she'd tell him as and when she felt able, and in turn he'd do his best with the touchy-feely stuff that she loved to discuss.

'Matt, when I saw you dying in that chair, I just knew that I wanted to die too. I never want to be away from you. Forgive me,' she whispered tantalisingly in his ear. She was trembling now - or was it he?

Just at that moment a thought crystallised that he realised he had known for some time.

She was now stronger than he, and he understood, too, in that sublime moment, that she loved him so much that she would never, ever reveal that she knew it to be so.

'I love you Sylvie. Thank you for waiting in time for me.'

'I love you too Matt. And it's been my pleasure.'

Though they were immersed in absolute darkness, the panorama overhead of the billions and billions of stars that could neither be imagined nor quantified, assured them of a bright future - one that would not only reach to the stars and back, but transcend time itself.

THE END